W9-BGV-906

The Ghost of Castle Kilgarrom

THE GHOST OF OF CASTLE KILGARROM

Jane Edwards

AVALON BOOKS
THOMAS BOUREGY AND COMPANY, INC.
401 LAFAYETTE STREET
NEW YORK, NEW YORK 10003

PRINTED IN THE UNITED STATES OF AMERICA
BY HADDON CRAFTSMEN, SCRANTON, PENNSYLVANIA

For Sheila and Dave, who waited a long time to see this in print.

And for Lucy Nott of London-town, who showed us the Emerald Isle, haunted castles and all.

CHAPTER ONE

Tara Delevan had her seat belt fastened by the time the jet began its long descent through the layers of clouds. Cinched in place, she squirmed in vain for her first glimpse of Ireland.

Suddenly, as though aware of her eagerness, the pilot banked the plane in an arcing turn. Tara caught a kaleidoscopic view of mist-shrouded trees, fields embroidered on the landscape like tiny patterns in a quilt, a lackadaisical thread of river. Seconds later the plane landed, and coasted down a wide tarmac runway toward a cluster of low buildings.

Jostling each other, chattering excitedly as they stretched for coats and hand luggage in the overhead storage racks, the passengers crowded down the aisle. More than a little nervous, Tara waited

1

for them to go on ahead. Not only was she six thousand miles away from home, but she was not sure, even yet, of the real purpose for which she had come. When asked, it had been easy enough to state that the trip was an unavoidable part of her job. In truth, however, a second purpose crowded constantly into her thoughts, far outweighing the first.

After the shrill melee of New York's JFK, the pace at Shannon Airport seemed leisurely, almost tranquil. Tara had nothing to declare. The uniformed customs officer took her at her word, casually rubber-stamping her crisp new passport. A second official squiggled a chalk mark along the outside of her suitcase.

So much for the complications of international travel. If it were all to be that easy. . . .

The tension of the past few days started to ebb as Tara slung her flight bag across her shoulder and followed the last straggling passengers toward the exit. She was here, in Ireland, and as soon as Neal appeared everything would be all right again. No more waiting for letters that didn't arrive. No more wondering why the few postcards she had received avoided all mention of Kilgarrom. Or Neal's family. Or when he would be returning to San Francisco.

Little shops, bursting with a bargain assortment of goods, beckoned from the other side of the long building. Tara's gray eyes bypassed them, focusing instead on the signs posted along the corridor, advertising tours of medieval castles and day trips to the Ring of Kerry. Some of the posters were printed in Gaelic. Seeing them, she felt a twinge of regret that she knew not one word of that language which looked so much more foreign than Spanish or French.

Supposing Neal's aunt spoke no English? But that was nonsense. Hadn't she read somewhere that the ancient Irish tongue had been outlawed for centuries and was only recently enjoying a revival?

Outside in the cobblestoned street, new arrivals greeted relatives or hailed taxicabs in an effort to escape the mist, which was rapidly turning to rain. Tara stared hopefully into the fast-dispersing throng, expecting at any minute to catch sight of her fiancé. With his springy auburn hair and strong, square chin, Neal would be hard to miss.

But only strangers returned her glance before they, too, disappeared. Suddenly the apprehension which had been playing tag with the back of her mind for over a week returned, full-fledged.

Tara set her suitcase down with a jolt. At once, raindrops blurred the squiggle of chalk. The overcast dreariness of the day seemed to crowd more closely around her. Flaxen feathers of hair, curled by the dampness, clustered about her forehead and ears. She smoothed them back, away from the swooping widow's peak that completed the heart shape of her small face, and rummaged for the waterproof hat her travel agent had insisted would come in handy.

What next, she wondered, trying to convince herself that the moisture in her eyes was caused only by the drizzle. Perhaps she should catch a bus straight for Dublin and get on with her job. That was the real reason she had come to Ireland— wasn't it? And if Neal didn't care enough. . . .

Before she could come to any firm decision, a blue car spurted up to the curb. A tall, lean man swathed in a tweed overcoat untangled himself from the gearshift and tumbled out, loping toward the terminal. His black brows were pulled together in annoyance. Tara saw him jerk a ferocious look at his wristwatch as he thrust past her.

In the act of pushing through the door he swung around as his eye caught and registered her presence.

"You'd not be Tara Delevan, would you?" The words came out abruptly, a curt demand softened only by the underlying brogue.

She stared up at him. "Yes, I—"

"Praise be to God!" he growled. "Come inside whilst we get this sorted out. Sure, and Caithlin'd call the wrath of the banshees down on my head if I left Neal's colleen out in this soft weather to catch her death."

Chagrin mixed with relief brought a flush to Tara's cheek. A stranger he might be, and rude in the bargain, but family names were reeling off his tongue. She hoisted her suitcase and surrendered it to him as they gained the shelter of the building.

"You seem to know all about me," she said cautiously. "Now—who are you?"

"What, has Neal never told you about his cousin Rory McDermott?" came back the mocking answer, quick as a thunderclap. The black eyebrows unknitted, and a hint of laughter crowded out the annoyance in his dark eyes. He fished in the depths of a pocket, dragging out a crumpled square of paper.

"The cable you sent, in case you have doubts about my authenticity." He handed it over. " 'Twas just delivered last night. It missed Neal altogether, worst luck. I was called away from Dublin to come and fetch you."

It was her cable, Tara saw, scanning the message she had sent from San Francisco. But it had been transmitted three days ago! She frowned, wishing she didn't have to kink her neck to look up at him. "What do you mean, 'it missed Neal altogether'? He's staying at Kilgarrom, isn't he?"

Nonchalantly, Rory hefted the suitcase. "Well, he is and he isn't," he replied, when they had scurried across the slick cobblestones and squeezed into the blue Rover. "It's business, he'll be telling you, that takes him here and there and all around the Republic. Looking for bits and pieces to import, like any clever American businessman."

There was a scornful turn to the last phrase. Tara was too elated to challenge it. No wonder Neal hadn't had time to write! He and his partner were struggling to establish their new import firm on the West Coast. Neal must have located a source of handcrafted items here in Ireland.

"How sensible of him," she said staunchly. "And even though he mightn't be expecting me, I'm sure he'll be delighted that I've come."

"Bound to be." Then the sarcasm ebbed from Rory's tone. "Forgive me, will you, if I haven't treated you as a loving cousin should. It's been a bit of a schemozzle all 'round, but now that you are here—*cead mile fáilte!* A hundred thousand welcomes."

Tara found herself smiling at the soft slur of Gaelic words. A more maddening man she had never met, yet what a lot of careless charm he had!

She resolved to atone for her inconvenient arrival by being an extra-pleasant guest. "Two of my grandparents came from Ireland," she told him spontaneously, as he shifted gears and sped away from the airport on the left side of the road. "Like Neal, my grandfather Delevan emigrated with his family when he was just a boy. His wife was an O'Brien from right here in County Clare."

"So that's how you came by the name." Rory's long, thin face was enlivened by an attractive grin. "Tara, the ancient home of the kings of Ireland."

"I was the only girl after four boys. My father insisted on calling me something special."

The mist-drenched landscape kept her enthralled for several miles. Rory obligingly slowed as they passed Bunratty Castle, a vast tower of stone six or seven hundred years old. Tourists, he said, instead of knights, partook of medieval banquets there nowadays. In contrast to that thoroughly restored landmark, the crumbled ruin of Macnamara's Castle hulked alongside the road, bringing visions of tragedy and dark deeds to Tara's imaginative mind.

The rain slashed down harder as they rolled across the bridge spanning the River Shannon, and through the gray little city of Limerick. "Is Kilgarrom much farther?" Tara asked eagerly.

"A hundred miles or so. American miles, not Irish, which are considerably longer. I'll have you there before nightfall."

Inside the car it had become rather steamy. Tara wound down the window an inch or two, and tugged the waterproof hat away from her hair. The movement drew Rory's attention. He glanced her way casually, then back at the road. But in a moment his dark gaze was back again, resting on her face with a puzzled frown.

His perplexed expression deepened as they

turned onto a highway marked in both Gaelic and English. "You remind me of someone. I can't think who," he finally explained.

Tara had been growing uncomfortable under his quizzical stare. "Oh, is that all? I was beginning to wonder whether the customs man had stamped 'Shannon' and the date on my forehead, as well as on my passport. I'm told I resemble my mother's family, who came from England."

The mocking tone returned to Rory's voice. "Ah, the broad-minded Americans! Here you'll seldom find Irish and English growing chummy enough to wed. Except in Ulster, of course, and even there...."

Ulster. That was Northern Ireland, where all the trouble had been taking place. Back home Tara had read the newspaper accounts of bombings and bloodshed, but such terrible happenings seemed very far removed from this peaceful land. To keep from snapping at Rory, she concentrated on the rural scenery. The Eire they were swiftly traversing appeared to be mostly tiny farms, their fields criss-crossed by the waist-high stone fences Rory had called hedgerows. Wild flowers brightened the roadside, and trout-filled streams ran alongside.

"Tell me about the family," she said, when the silence had stretched to an uncomfortable length. "I know that Neal's mother died when he was a boy, and his father several years ago. Then last month he received word that his Uncle Cormac had drowned. Are you and Aunt Caithlin the only relatives he has left?"

Rory nodded. "We are. Unusual in an Irish family, which as a rule sprawls over six counties, but that's the truth of it. There were only three Fitzgarths in the last generation—Cormac and his two younger sisters—and those lucky to survive. One of the girls was my mother. The other produced Neal. To their great sorrow, Cormac and Caithlin had no children."

What a tragedy for a proud old family, Tara reflected. "So the direct line died out," she mused aloud. "And now Kilgarrom goes to—"

"To the nephews, of course, with the proviso that Caithlin be cared for." A taunting grin touched Rory's somber face. "Had you visions of becoming mistress of Kilgarrom? 'Twas a grand place once, I'll warrant you."

"It could be Buckingham Palace, for all I'd care! Do you imagine I've come all this distance to snatch away a poor old widow's home?"

Sparks crackled in her eyes until she caught sight of the quirk at the corners of Rory's mouth. She reddened, feeling more like an adolescent given to tantrums than a grown woman of twenty-three. She would simply have to learn to cope with this abrasive man without losing her temper!

In the driver's seat Rory was chuckling openly. "I'll admit that the notion did occur to me. That was one of the reasons I was so infuriated at having to drive clear across the country to collect you. Why are you here, then? Worried about the boyfriend?"

"Not at all!"

Tara sat up straighter, loathe to admit just how concerned she had become at the infrequency of Neal's postcards and the inexplicable way he kept delaying his return to California.

"I've a job to finish," she said, "and the information I need isn't available in the States. Searching out family trees is an interesting occupation, but it requires a great deal of research."

Rory's black brows tilted. "So it's a genealogist we have with us. That's a fine profession, back-tracking people's lineage and identifying all their grand ancestors in the history books."

"And shuffling into the background those who died in debtors' prisons or were hanged as horse thieves!"

He seemed more nettled than amused. "Then I was wasting my breath, telling you about Cormac Fitzgarth. No doubt you have the family neatly cross-indexed, clear back to the time the Vikings sailed their longboats into Waterford harbor?"

Tara started to explain that in the few months she and Neal had known each other, she had learned practically nothing about his family. Then she checked her words. That was certainly none of Rory's concern.

"No," she replied evenly. "We've been concentrating mostly on the future. Perhaps someday I'll chart out Neal's ancestry to amuse our children. Then Cormac and Caithlin will play a part in the family tree."

"Speaking of Caithlin, I wouldn't call her a 'poor old widow,'" Rory said. "She's sixty or thereabouts, and a bit daft, but well respected by everyone in spite of that."

"Daft? You mean eccentric?" Tara shrugged. "All of us have at least one relative who's considered a trifle peculiar."

"Oh, certainly. Still—" Rory hesitated, guarding his tongue, then barged ahead impatiently, as though determined to say what had to be said and be done with it. "It's only because you're practically a member of the family that I'm telling you this, mind. Caithlin...believes in ghosts. One, at least. If you bother to ask, she'll tell you Kilgarrom is haunted."

Tara eyed him skeptically. Mockery again? But he appeared to be dead serious. His gaze, as he removed it from the road and met her stare, had a "take it or leave it" finality.

Their eyes collided. His widened abruptly, then narrowed to slits, masking a flicker of some new emotion. The expression darted in and out too quickly for Tara to fathom its meaning, but whatever it was had a definitely unsettling effect on Rory. His grip on the wheel slackened, and the Rover swerved halfway into the oncoming lane.

Fortunately, the road ahead was empty. He jerked the wheel back, muttering a word or two of Gaelic. It didn't sound like the kind of language one learned in church.

It took Tara a moment to regain her breath. "What on earth is the matter?" she asked. "You looked as though *you* had seen a ghost."

"In a manner of speaking, I did." Rory lifted a swooping eyebrow in her direction, this time keeping both hands clenched on the steering wheel. "Nothing to trouble you, understand. It's just that I've suddenly remembered who you reminded me of."

"Who?"

"You'll see—when we reach Kilgarrom."

There seemed little to be said after that. Tara ventured a question now and then and learned, through monosyllabic answers, that Rory owned a Dublin bookshop and was an enthusiastic weekend fisherman. But his bantering tone was gone, and with it all the fun and challenge of the conversation.

Vaguely uneasy, she avoided his rigid profile, staring out instead at deep crystal lakes and purple, triangular hills. She hadn't imagined that such a quiet, empty, peaceful land still existed anywhere on earth.

The road narrowed and wound and narrowed again before they reached the outskirts of the village of Ballycroom. One unpaved street meandered the length of the town. Along it hopscotched tiny shops and equally small dwellings, their windows masked by lace curtains. But here and there half-doors swung open in a neighborly way, and in the miniature patch of lawn bordering each cottage daisies poked white heads against the green blades of grass.

A pub stood at the head of the row, a post office in the middle. On the outer edge the church's spire appeared to push protectively upward against the clouds.

"I like it!" Tara had a hunch that such words as "quaint" and "picturesque" were best kept to herself. "Does the thatch on the roofs keep the cottages warm inside?"

"Warm enough—if everyone clusters 'round the hearth."

Rory's voice sounded cheerier now. He guided the car around a sharp curve, which instantly blotted Ballycroom from sight and just as quickly brought into view one of the most beautiful lakes Tara had ever seen. It was wide and indigo blue, with trees rimming its perimeter and serene islands anchored in the center.

"Lough Duneen," Rory commented. "Now, look up—clear up the hill."

Tall trees crowded the steep, rutted lane giving access to Kilgarrom. At first Tara could see nothing but a gloom of shadows hulking close together at the top. Then a turret appeared, thin and round and stone, higher than the steeple of any church. From it stretched an expanse of bare red brick, connected, far beyond that, to a second turret. A cobblestoned courtyard took the place of lawn. Not a vine, not even a flower softened the stark facade of the vast structure.

"Good heavens!" Tara said. "No wonder Caithlin believes in ghosts!"

She stepped from the car, apprehension rising. An elderly woman, shawl clutched around her head, hobbled toward them.

Rory lifted her suitcase from the Rover's "boot" as though, having fulfilled his duty in collecting her from the airport, he could not wait to be rid of her.

"Evening, Brigid," he called. "Here's Tara Delevan, all the way from Shannon safe and sound."

Tara stepped forward to smile a timid greeting at the housekeeper. Wisps of frost-white hair frizzled out from beneath the shawl. Below it, the brow and cheeks were furrowed with a road map of lines and wrinkles. Celt-blue eyes, as keen and penetrating as any wary animal's, appraised the girl.

"Cead mile fáilte."

Her stern lips made short work of the "hundred thousand welcomes." Tara murmured her thanks, feeling not at all welcome, and wondered if the wrinkled skin were always so pale. Or had it blanched since she moved nearer?

They hurried around to the side door, to enter a

kitchen warmed by a huge, black coal stove. Before Tara could more than glance around, Rory moved swiftly across the room, tossing orders back over his shoulder.

"Take Tara up to her room, will you? I'll return to fetch the suitcase as soon as I've had a word with Caithlin."

A word of warning, Tara thought intuitively. But why should it be necessary?

Brigid picked up a kerosene lantern and headed up a flight of wooden stairs. Beneath the thin soles of her traveling pumps, Tara could feel the grooves worn by generations of servants' feet. There were a great many steps for only one flight; the high ceilings of the ground-floor rooms accounted for that, she supposed.

In the upper hall burned three candlelit chandeliers, swaying with the motion of their passing. Under the film that had accumulated over the years they appeared to be real Waterford crystal. Crystal or not, Tara was grateful for the wan glow they emitted. The dark corridor seemed to go on and on.

At last Brigid halted and flung open a door. The room they entered was large enough to house a medium-sized family. The four-poster bed looked comfortable, as did the worn armchair near the window. A lamp rested on a low table, waiting to be lit.

"Thank you so much." Tara tried to ignore the swift, quickly withdrawn glances the old woman kept darting in her direction. "Keeping up even one room this size must be hard work for you. I'll try not to cause any bother."

"Bathroom's three doors farther along." Brigid

gave no answering smile. "You'll be wanting a meal. Come down when you're ready."

Tara's first impulse upon being left alone was to stretch across the bed and catnap for about sixteen hours. Her head buzzed from the disorienting effects of jet lag. The long drive across Ireland had added a second layer of exhaustion.

She sank down for a moment, massaging her throbbing brow. What a baffling day it had been! No Neal, only a resentful cousin to meet her. Next, an outright warning that Kilgarrom's mistress maintained a nodding acquaintance with ghosts. And finally, the bizarre reaction her own appearance had seemed to evoke, first in Rory and then in Brigid.

A hundred thousand welcomes indeed!

Tara got up wearily, telling herself that she needn't stay. Tomorrow she could catch a bus to Dublin and get on with her job. If Neal wanted to join her there—

But perhaps things would seem less bewildering by daylight. She made her way to the turn-of-the-century bathroom and felt somewhat better after splashing cold water across her face. The mirror above the sink was speckled with black dots where the mercury had worn away, but it was still capable of showing a clear reflection. More than ever now, Tara wondered who her "look-alike" could be. The other girl must have gray eyes under level and determined brows, and a heart-shaped face framed by very fair hair. Freckles too?

She coped briskly with the hairbrush, then brushed some powder along the sprinkle of golden flecks marching across the bridge of her nose.

As Tara emerged into the hall, a murmur of

voices caught her ear. Curious, she took a few
steps to the right. More shadows than light filled
the corridor, but by the farthest-reaching rays of
the center chandelier she made out the sweeping
curve of an elegant staircase. Warm lamplight
glowed below.

A man's voice rumbled somewhere down there
on the ground floor. Tara's breath caught in her
throat. Maybe Neal.... She plunged downward,
the tap of her steps muffled by the tattered runner
flowing underfoot. Hope died as, halfway down,
she caught sight of Rory. He was speaking earnestly to a slim, straight-backed woman who stood
nearly as tall as he. A crown of braids, white with
black patches in them, like swirls of chocolate in a
marble cake, added to her height.

Tara hesitated, reluctant to interrupt yet unwill-
ing, having come this far, to return to the cold and
gloomy upper floor. Descending more slowly, she
saw outlined on the front wall a pair of massive
entrance doors, high and wide enough for a
mounted horseman to ride through into the foyer.
When she paused on the bottom step, the contours
of a gilt-framed portrait on the opposite wall came
into view.

"It's incredible, I tell you," Rory was saying.
"You'd best be prepared—"

Tara must have moved; either that or intuition
drew his eyes in her direction. He bit back the next
words. The woman beside him turned questioningly
toward the stairs.

Even from twenty feet away Tara had no trouble
identifying the play of expression across the
woman's face. It changed quickly from interest to

mild surprise, then to a mixture of shock and terror.

The white lips moved soundlessly; the woman's eyes fluttered shut. Before Rory could leap forward to break her fall, she crumpled to the floor at his feet!

CHAPTER TWO

For a stunned moment nobody moved. Then Tara darted forward, dropping to her knees beside the limp figure. She pushed up one long sleeve of the dress, and with shaking fingers fumbled for a pulse in the thin wrist.

To her relief it was beating steadily. "It's all right. She's only fainted."

Rory stooped down, smoothing back a few wisps that had floated loose from the crown of braids. With surprising tenderness he lifted the unconscious woman and carried her over to a spindle-legged sofa near the door.

But there was nothing tender in the way he confronted Tara. "Of all the daft things to do!" he shouted. "Appearing like that, and frightening poor Caithlin half out of her wits!"

17

Tara blazed back at him in justified fury. "I didn't just *appear*. I *walked* down the stairs! Who did she think I was?"

In answer, he gestured toward the painting. "Her name was Drucilla Fitzgarth."

Still irate, Tara looked up—and caught her breath. Lamplight threw a soft, flattering glow on the portrait, erasing cracks of age and bringing small details into focus. The model was clad in a gown that was two or three centuries out of date, but there any disparity ended. Fair hair swooped back from a deep widow's peak. The forehead was smooth and high and marked by straight, uncompromising brows above eyes the color of slate. There was the merest tilt to the small nose. While the lips were touched by a slight smile, the round cheeks diminished into a stubbornly pointed chin. It was like gazing into an old, old mirror. The only thing missing was the freckles.

"Why—why didn't you tell me?"

"What was I to say? 'Pardon me, Miss Delevan, would it interest you to know that you bear an uncanny resemblance to our family ghost?' You'd have thought me demented. Besides—"

A flutter of motion from the sofa diverted the argument. Tara turned guiltily and saw Caithlin Fitzgarth's pale blue eyes fixed on her. The terror had vanished, though her slender face was still chalk white.

"Rory is not to blame for my foolishness. You seemed so like the Lady with the Harp—"

Assisted by Rory, Caithlin managed to sit up. She brushed her full skirt out of the way, and motioned for Tara to sit beside her. "How distressing that we should meet in this way. My nephew did his best to save me embarrassment, yet see how I reacted!"

"I'm to blame, for interrupting. I had no idea...." Tara's eyes swiveled back to the portrait. She saw now that there was a small Irish harp on the model's lap. Delicate fingers were slightly curved, ready to pluck at the strings. "It's truly amazing! But surely Neal must have remarked on the resemblance?"

Caithlin shook her head. "The painting was only resurrected from the attic this week. Himself had banished it there years ago, in the hope that if it were no longer in plain sight—"

Tactfully, Rory filled the awkward pause by complaining of hunger and thirst. He shot a glance at Tara as he helped his aunt to her feet. "I told you so," his look seemed to say.

He had been serious, back there in the car, she realized now. The portrait's eyes seemed to follow as she turned to move away. Rory's earlier remarks made it easy to understand why Cormac Fitzgarth had wanted the painting hidden away. No one needed to tell her that it was Drucilla who still haunted Kilgarrom.

Haunted it for Caithlin, at least. Or did Rory also believe?

She thrust the uncomfortable question aside, looking around with interest at the rooms they passed. What dim light radiated from the chandeliers high overhead afforded fleeting glimpses of a vast and forlorn down-at-the-heelsness. Dampness and a faint odor of mold pervaded Kilgarrom. It was too old, too massive to be thought of as a home.

Tara felt more at ease in the plain, no-nonsense

kitchen. A fire roared in the stove; Brigid hobbled around giving orders as to who was to sit where.

The thought of a see-through Drucilla roaming the halls was better than envisioning some horrid old ogre in chains, she admitted whimsically to herself when they sat down to a meal of barley soup, soda bread fresh from the oven, and cups of strong, blowtorch-hot tea. But what little she had seen of Caithlin seemed not the least bit "daft." It must have taken more than an old legend to convince Neal's aunt that not all the inhabitants of Kilgarrom were made of flesh and blood.

"The family ghost," Rory had called Drucilla. The occult had never appealed to Tara. Twenty-four hours ago she would have scoffed at anyone who talked of specters and haunted houses. Yet here, with the mist hemming this dilapidated castle off from the rest of the world, the idea seemed much less farfetched.

Gradually the color returned to Caithlin's cheeks. Brigid continued to shuffle grumpily about the room, bringing what was needed to the table and removing the plates when they had been emptied. No amount of urging could persuade her to sit down with them.

While waiting for her second cup of tea to cool, Tara picked up a wide silver ring on which the soup tureen had rested earlier.

Rory flicked it with his fingernail. "In even the poorest Irish home you're likely to come across a bit of old silver. The making of things such as this was quite a craft in the old days. This was made to hold a steaming punch bowl, though modern collectors are apt to call it a napkin ring."

A network of tiny scratches betrayed the silver's

age. As Tara examined the exquisite craftsmanship of the piece, it caught the light in its curve and reflected her image back at her. Quickly she replaced it on the table. Now she knew why she had been concentrating on the question of ghosts for the past half hour. That subject was easier to accept than the bewildering likeness between her own face and the one in the portrait.

It was true, what she had told Rory, that she knew practically nothing of Neal's heritage. Yet she was very well acquainted with the history of her own ancestors. Neither the Delevans nor the O'Briens had come from this part of Ireland; her first success as a fledgling genealogist had been to trace their lineage back several centuries. It was highly unlikely that Drucilla could have been even a remote kinswoman of theirs. And her mother's forebears had come from England.

Yet there must be some rational explanation!

If only it were Neal rather than Rory seated in the next chair. He would have made light of things supernatural; would have pointed out the good and the beautiful to be seen in the house, and eased her fatigue with kisses and blarney.

Caithlin had mentioned bringing the portrait back downstairs "this week," Tara remembered. So Neal had been gone for longer than a day or two. She looked across the table at his aunt.

"How difficult this must be for you," Tara said, "having a stranger arrive with only a few hours' notice. Please believe I never would have imposed if I hadn't thought Neal would be here. Is he expected back soon?"

"God willing," Caithlin replied. "It's to County Galway they've gone this time, to see the sweaters the fishermen's womenfolk knit out on the Aran Islands. There's a market for such goods in America, Neal was telling me. But no matter. You're welcome here, child, for as long as you can stay."

Touched by the invitation, Tara glanced past Caithlin to see Brigid posed by the sink in a listening attitude. Her back was rigid with disapproval. For some reason she did not share Caithlin's hospitable attitude. Perhaps she felt an extra person in the house would create more work.

Tomorrow, Tara decided, she would show her that Americans were no idlers who needed to be waited on. Tonight, though, she could not have washed a dish without letting it slip through her tired fingers. Even lifting the teacup was becoming an effort.

"You're much too kind," she said. "Would you mind if I went to bed now? My system is still on Pacific Coast time, which means that at home it's nearly time to get up."

"To think of such a thing! Rest well, then."

Rory pushed back his chair, announcing that he would carry the suitcase upstairs for her. The next moment he was moving easily through the maze of turnings, past the lifeless, dust-sheeted rooms, to the central staircase. Tara hesitated on the bottom step for another look at the woman in the portrait. Again, she wondered what unknown bond existed between them. Mere chance had not created two faces so nearly identical. The notion of a common heritage shared by Drucilla and herself was definitely intriguing.

Before she left Kilgarrom, Tara resolved, she would discover the link that lay between them.

Rory deposited the heavy carryall in the doorway of her room. She caught his sleeve before he could turn away. "I never did thank you for driving all that distance," she said. "Will you be staying on or returning to Dublin?"

"Returning, for a time. I've a bookshop to run, as I told you. But it isn't far. I'll be back on the weekend." His voice slipped back into its old mocking tone as he glanced at the diamond sparkling on her finger. "By that time you and my cousin will doubtless be enjoying your reunion. Sure, and he's likely to even forget business, now that you've come."

"I wouldn't be surprised," Tara said, as coolly as she was able. "Goodnight, Rory."

Within minutes after his footsteps had faded away Tara was ready for bed. For some contrary reason the lure of sleep was less pressing now. She blew out the lamp. Then, leaving the candles burning in their sconces, she moved over to one of the tall windows and pushed aside the draperies. She tugged up the lower half of the window and leaned out, welcoming the damp night air on her face.

In this northerly latitude twilight was slow in fading. Salmon streaks, left over from the sunset, mingled with the charcoal clouds overhead. They sparked a warm reflection in the quiet lake far below. It was a magnificent view, beautiful and silent. Lonely too. Living here, Tara decided, out of sight of the rest of the world, it would not be hard to lose touch with the present and slide back into the past.

A blur of movement caught her eye as she was about to pull her head inside. Hesitating, she saw a large gray beast trot into view. The Irish wolfhound halted to stare down at the motionless waters of

Lough Duneen. With him on sentry duty, she thought, no outsiders would dare disturb Kilgarrom.

It wasn't until she had snuffed out the candles and drawn the quilts up under her chin that Tara remembered that the castle was reputed to be haunted. A threat, if there were one, would likely come from inside the walls, not without.

What nonsense! she told herself, rolling over. Caithlin was welcome to her Lady with the Harp. For her own part, the most important thing was that she would soon be seeing Neal again.

Then drowsily, half awake, she frowned, remembering Caithlin's words. "It's to County Galway they've gone this time." What was so engrossing about Aran sweaters that they could keep Neal away for days on end? And . . . *they?*

Sleep overtook her before she could puzzle out the disturbing pronoun.

CHAPTER THREE

The sun was high overhead when Tara awoke. She had not drawn the draperies the previous night. Now, warm shafts of daylight poked inquisitive fingers into every corner of the room. Even the shabby furnishings had a mellower look. No doubt the rest of Kilgarrom would seem different, too, now that golden sunshine had replaced the shadows of dusk.

While bathing and dressing, Tara reflected on the events of the evening before. How out of proportion everything had seemed then. Disappointment, fatigue, and Rory's nonsensical tongue had all too easily opened the way for power of suggestion to affect her. And one glimpse of an antique portrait had startled her imagination into galloping ahead of common sense. But a deep, long sleep had restored her perspective. Spooked the spirits, so to speak.

25

Tara tidied her bed, then ran down the worn rear stairs to the kitchen. There she found a girl with a plump, pretty face and a mop of orange-red hair coping with the balky old coal burner.

"Ah, miss," she exclaimed, wiping her sooty fingers on her apron. "It's burning at last, I do believe. Quick, tell me how you like your eggs before this black-hearted monster coughs itself into another fit!"

"Scrambled." Tara said, laughing. "Do you go through this every day?"

"More's the pity." She was Molly Breen from Ballycroom, the girl added. Five mornings a week she bicycled up from the village to lend a hand.

"This must have been a lovely morning to be out in the fresh air," Tara said, "but I imagine that pedaling up that steep hill is no fun when it rains. Wouldn't it be easier to stay here during the week and just go home to Ballycroom on your days off?"

Molly tossed her bright mop and suddenly became very absorbed at the sink. "'Tisn't so awfully far."

No doubt, Tara thought perceptively, the story of Drucilla's reappearances had spread to the village. Molly was probably taking no chances of meeting the Lady with the Harp in a darkened hall.

A couple of sharp barks at the kitchen door spared her the effort of changing the subject. "That'll be Gray Boy," Molly said, clearly glad of the diversion. "I'll let him in, shall I, and fix his food?"

"Of course." Tara had no fear of animals. She set her dishes on the counter. As she had expected, it was the large wolfhound she had spotted the evening before who came trotting in to be fed. Waiting until he had finished gulping down the food Molly set out for him, she then approached him quietly and proceeded to make friends. Gray Boy was deigning to have his ears scratched by the time Caithlin walked into the room.

Her smile was warm as she greeted her guest. "I see there's no need to ask if you rested well. How pretty you look this morning, my dear!"

"It's all due to your comfortable bed," Tara replied cheerfully. "After a sleep like that, I feel as if I can even face Rory without squabbling."

Looking amused, Caithlin suggested she hold the suggestion for a few days, since her younger nephew had returned to Dublin early that morning. "Which leaves the two of us time to get acquainted. Is there anything special you'd like to do today?"

"Could you show me around Kilgarrom? I've never been inside a castle before."

The older woman seemed pleased by the request. "Most of the house was built in the mid-1700s," she said, leading the way down the hall. "But Kilgarrom itself goes back about five hundred years before that. It was a true castle fortress to begin with, built to defend this part of the country against invaders."

It was hard for an American to picture any structure still standing after such a long history. "Did it belong to the family even in those early times?"

Caithlin nodded. "A Fitzgarth helped the great Irish king, Brian Boru, drive the Vikings from our shores in 1014. One of his descendants built Kilgarrom about two hundred years later, during Norman times. Until the middle of the 1650s, the clan lived here undisturbed. Then Cromwell's armies descended on the land, bent on destroying everything in Ireland. Their cannon blazed away at the walls until there was little left except the turrets and the great keep. 'Twas a time of terrible oppression and religious persecution."

Tara was familiar with Ireland's grim history. For a span of nearly four hundred years the people were mercilessly taxed. Catholics were forbidden to hold public office, or even to vote.

"How did they manage to rebuild Kilgarrom?" she asked.

Their walk had taken them as far as the central foyer. Here had stood the ancient keep, the very heart of the castle. Caithlin gazed reminiscently around at the old walls, which in this part of the house were built of the original stone.

"A youth named Kevin Fitzgarth decided to avenge his family for all they had suffered," she said. "He made his way to Dublin. There he kidnapped a beautiful English girl, and held her for ransom. Her people were fabulously wealthy. Kevin asked a fortune many times over for her safe return. But by the time the ransom was paid he had fallen in love with the girl, and she with him. They fled back here, to Kilgarrom. Drucilla herself supervised the rebuilding of the castle with the money her family had paid."

Drucilla! Tara's heart beat faster. She turned to stare at the painted face so mysteriously like her own. "Didn't her father try to find them?"

"And find them he did, after several years' searching," Caithlin said. "Up the hill he and his soldiers came, one dark, blustery night, without a moment's warning. Kevin took his stand at the door. 'Tis said Drucilla watched the horrible scene from that very staircase. When Kevin fell, run through with her father's own sword, she snatched up her twin boys and managed to escape through a secret passageway."

"Poor thing! She must have been wild with grief."

"She stayed in hiding until her father's troops had left. Then she set about destroying everything that had any connection with her own kin. Not once in the fifty years between then and the time she died did Drucilla ever acknowledge that English blood ran in her veins."

Tara swung around, appalled. "You mean you don't know *who* she was? There wasn't any clue at all left?"

"Nothing. Drucilla was an excellent harpist, and a letter one of her sons wrote many years later described her as having a sweet and lovely voice. Some of the songs she composed about her lost love were written down. I believe the original copies are still up in the attic. But there was never a mention of her own people in any of the verses."

"How disappointing!"

About to ask whether the secret passageway still existed, Tara paused. From outside in the courtyard came the muffled growl of a car engine. Seconds later one of the thick, carved doors was flung open. A young man with auburn hair strode jauntily inside.

"Neal!"

In no time at all Tara was across the foyer and encircled by his arms. "You're six thousand miles away—aren't you?" Neal exclaimed, when at last they drew apart. "I can't believe what I'm seeing! Why didn't you let me know you were coming?"

"I tried, but my cable must have been delayed.

Rory picked me up in Shannon, and Caithlin said you were in Galway. . . ."

Tara's voice trailed off. For the first time she became aware that Neal had not arrived alone. Behind him, poised in the doorway with the grace of a fashion model, stood the most beautiful young woman she had ever seen.

"Hello. I'm Eileen O'Keefe." The woman moved forward, shrugging a cascade of long, midnight black hair over her shoulders. Her eyes, beneath their sooty fringe of lashes, were green as shamrocks, and a mini-dimple winked at the corner of her mouth.

Warily, Tara introduced herself in turn. Sensing her distress, Caithlin stepped forward with an affectionate greeting for both newcomers. She linked arms with Eileen and drew her tactfully away, saying, "Come and have a cup of tea. How was the sweater hunting in Aran?"

"Yes," Tara said mockingly, when they were out of earshot. "How was the sweater hunting?"

"Not nearly so exciting as finding you here, *alannah*," Neal declared forthrightly. He was stockier than his cousin and several inches shorter. Tara forgot to be angry and settled for letting him wrap her close to his strong frame. When finally he raised his head again, her lips tingled with the delicious pressure he'd applied.

"Tell me," he murmured, "what are you doing in Ireland? Run out of family trees to chart in San Francisco?"

"Just the opposite. I've been commissioned to do a fascinating genealogy. A man named Matthew Ardill wants to give his parents a unique gift for their golden wedding anniversary—as complete a charting of their lineage as I can concoct. The mother's ancestors arrived on the Mayflower, so that was no real problem, and I've managed to trace his father's line back seven generations. I'm stymied at the point where the emigrating ancestor crossed the Atlantic. Mr. Ardill paid my airfare so I could continue the research over here."

Neal grinned. "Sounds like a good fellow. Then it wasn't me you came to see, after all?"

"Didn't you ever hear of combining business with pleasure?" Tara laced her fingers through his, and swiveled so that he could see the portrait on the wall. "I haven't started digging into the Ardills' records yet. But look what I did find."

Neal whistled in astonishment. "Not your old gran?"

"Yours, actually. A dozen times great-great." Tara repeated the dramatic tale of how Kevin Fitz-garth had brought Drucilla to Kilgarrom. "Her maiden name is a mystery. According to Rory, Drucilla is still in residence—in spirit, at least."

"That fool cousin of mine would say anything!" Neal growled in exasperation. "What did he tell you about Cormac?"

"Hardly anything." Tara glanced at him in surprise. "I gathered that your uncle had a tragic childhood. Rory said he and his sisters were lucky to survive. And that Cormac had left Kilgarrom to the two of you."

"Not exactly, but that's close enough." For some unaccountable reason, Neal seemed relieved. "It hardly matters because the place is to be sold as soon as we can find a buyer. Between livestock and land and this great barn of a house, we should net enough to keep Caithlin in comfort for the rest of her life."

Tara wondered if his aunt knew of this plan. Certainly Rory hadn't indicated that Kilgarrom was soon to change hands. "Why didn't you write and tell me what was going on here? I was starting to get worried."

"Oh, the family problems seemed too complicated to describe in a letter," Neal said lightly. "Besides, I've been chasing all over the Republic, looking at handcrafted goods and placing orders for shipment home. Eileen has been a marvelous help. She's steered me onto bargains I never could have hoped to find by myself."

"How nice," Tara replied, with less than her usual enthusiasm. "Then you'll be ready to come home soon?"

"Soon—I hope." Neal stopped further questions with a kiss.

Over tea, Tara gathered that Eileen was a successful businesswoman. She created new fabric designs for other women who did their weaving at home. These cottage industry products were merchandized to coat and suit makers in the large cities.

Eileen turned the discussion to Tara's career. "Neal tells me you are a genealogist. Are you here to work on an assignment?"

Matthew Ardill's commission was discussed in detail. "My client is anxious to know something about his father's early ancestors. I hope to find a birth record for the Liam Ardill who emigrated to America, and trace the family back from that point."

"Naturally, you'll need to go to Dublin to do that," Eileen said.

But Caithlin was wrinkling her forehead. "Perhaps not. Molly, wasn't Annie Mullins an Ardill?"

"Ardill, Ardhill, something like that. Her mother lives out on the farm with Annie and Seamus; she could tell you sure." Molly's eyes danced with a lively interest. "Oh, miss, wouldn't it be lucky if you could find the very folks you need right there in the village?"

"Not lucky—a miracle," Tara said, curbing her enthusiasm. "By the time you've traced a family back several generations, you discover that their relationships have become terribly confused. Nephews were referred to as 'cousins,' and in-laws as plain 'daughter' or 'son.' And sometimes people didn't bother to register births anywhere except in their family Bibles. So trying to find the direct line of descent can be extremely tricky."

Neal squeezed her fingers. "Without a challenge you wouldn't find it half so much fun. Think what a field day you'll have with all those old records in the capital."

"No need to rush off," Caithlin said easily. "Eileen can run you over for a chat with Annie Mullins and her mother tomorrow, if you like."

Tara agreed this sounded like a logical starting point. Looking around the table, she wondered why only Caithlin seemed in favor of having her follow up on the local family.

If she didn't know better, she'd almost have thought that Neal was eager for her to leave Kilgarrom!

CHAPTER FOUR

For the rest of the day, the members of the house went around being extremely polite to one another. In between, Eileen looked watchful, while Neal lapsed often into bouts of preoccupation. Tara vacillated between wishing that Eileen would go home to wherever it was she lived, and yearning to haul her fiancé back to America where they both belonged.

Even Caithlin looked relieved when evening came and good nights could be exchanged. Alone for the first time since their reunion in the foyer, Neal saw Tara to her bedroom door.

"Sleep well," he said, kissing her solemnly.

"You too." Neal looked tired and worried, Tara thought, like a man who could do with eight or ten hours' slumber.

35

Her own rest was disturbed by odd dreams in which everyone carried harps. The hands of her small travel alarm clock were pointing to six-thirty by the time she came fully awake and decided that further sleep was a lost cause. Hoping that the tense atmosphere of the previous day would have disappeared as completely as the night's chimeras, she climbed quickly out of bed and pulled on slim-legged slacks and a long-sleeved shirt that was both warm and becoming.

Brigid's fretful voice could be heard as she slipped down the back stairs. About to continue on into the kitchen, Tara's ears picked up her own name. She halted in embarrassment.

"...don't like letting that girl stay here," the old woman was grousing. "She'll bring bad luck on the house like the one before her did. Peas in a pod for looks, and foreigners as well, for all this one claims to have Irish blood in her veins."

"What other kind could it be, with a name like Tara Delevan?" came Caithlin's amused reply.

Red-cheeked, Tara retreated hastily to a point halfway up the stairs. At least she knew now why Brigid had seemed to take an instant dislike to her. Drucilla had brought disaster to Kilgarrom. Since Tara bore a striking resemblance to Kevin Fitzgarth's stolen bride, Brigid feared that another catastrophe might strike.

Shaking her head at such superstitious nonsense, she started down again, this time taking care that her footsteps were loud enough to announce her arrival. Caithlin, in a warm quilted robe, her hair loosely plaited, looked up from the table with every evidence of pleasure as her American visitor stepped through the door.

"Just the person I wanted to see. Come help me settle on a menu," she said. "I'm expecting a large group of visitors in a few days."

Avoiding Brigid's eyes, Tara dropped into a chair. "How large?"

"Fifteen or twenty. They'll be staying just the one night," Caithlin explained.

It was still mind-boggling to Tara to think of a house large enough to accommodate such a crowd. She suggested a buffet supper as being the simplest method of feeding a throng of that size. "Set it all out on a long table and let the people help themselves."

"Splendid!" Caithlin said, deciding quickly on a ham, rolls, and several salads. "All the work can be done ahead of time."

Brigid slammed the teapot on the table. "What Father O'Dea would have to say about such heathen goings-on, I hardly dare think!"

Confused, Tara asked who it was that Caithlin was expecting.

"I hope you won't also think me a silly old woman, my dear." Neal's aunt shot a slightly defiant glance at her housekeeper. "They are members of a spiritualist society from London. Quite a lot of intelligent people do believe in a world outside of our material one, you know. Even Brigid puts food out on the step on All Hallows' Eve."

"That's a different matter altogether," Brigid declared, with a toss of her shawl. She stumped out of the room, leaving Caithlin looking relieved.

"The arrangements for the society's visit were made last week," Caithlin explained. "They've been wanting to come for years, but Cormac—

Well, he didn't encourage such things. I see no reason why they shouldn't try to catch a glimpse of Drucilla if she's willing to show herself. Perhaps one of them can think of a way to pacify her. Let her rest at last."

In spite of her growing affection for Neal's aunt, Tara felt an icy shiver wiggle up her spine. "When are they coming?"

"Friday. Two nights from now." Caithlin stirred sugar into her tea, and poured a cup for Tara. "There are other haunted castles in Ireland," she said seriously. "Kildare, for example, has been turned into a hotel, yet inexplicable tales about the tower room persist. Not even hardheaded scientists can explain some of the manifestations known to have taken place there."

"Well..." Tara said, then laughed. "I suppose it's no wilder than trying to find out if you're related to someone who died centuries ago. I'll help you prepare for the guests. Just so long as I don't have to believe in anything that happens!"

"Do you want to take a run over to the Mullins farm before lunch?" Eileen asked later that morning.

Rather surprised, Tara agreed at once. "Love to, if you don't mind driving me."

"Might as well get it over with," Eileen said in a resigned way.

"I agree," Tara replied coolly. "I'll be ready to go in a minute."

Upstairs, she slipped on a pair of walking shoes and collected the Ardill folder from her suitcase. Then she hurried down the corridor to Neal's room, hoping he might be persuaded to come along.

Reluctantly he shook his head. "Sorry, hon, but I've got to go see Tim Foyle, the stableman. There's a horse fair being held not far from here this weekend. If we can get the animals ready in time, this would be a good opportunity to sell off some of Kilgarrom's stock."

It saddened Tara to think of everything going, piece by piece. "Have you talked this over with Caithlin?"

He nodded. "She doesn't really want to stay on here, now that Cormac's gone. Rory is supposed to be putting the house into the hands of a realtor, but so far we've not been contacted."

Eileen was waiting outside in a powerful little red MG. They whizzed through Ballycroom; within a few minutes she turned up a lane leading to a well-kept dairy farm.

Neither Annie nor her mother, much to their regret, was able to add anything to the information Tara had already compiled on the Liam Eugene Ardill who had arrived in the United States on May 16, 1847.

"We've kin who emigrated to America, but it was years later than that," Annie said. "And of course Mother's family spelled the name Ardell."

Mrs. Ardell peered nearsightedly at the genealogical chart Tara was displaying. "Fancy that! You've even learned the name of the boat he sailed over on. 'Twas a coffin ship, I'll warrant. Not everyone who got on, got off alive."

This Tara knew only too well. "Still," she said, "it must have seemed worth the risk to try and escape the famine conditions here."

"The family's done well in America, has it?" Annie asked.

"Yes, indeed. My client is head of an engineering company in California."

"Isn't that awfully frustrating?" Eileen asked, after they had thanked the women and headed back. "Having a promising lead come to nothing?"

"Sure. But when you're through moaning you try another sourcebook, or a different relative—or you ruin your shoes prowling around a cemetery, hoping to find a clue on a faded tombstone." Tara smiled to show she took it in stride. "Have you ever tried digging into your own family's history?"

"I prefer to think about tomorrow, not yester-day," Eileen retorted, and she pushed down harder on the accelerator.

About four o'clock Neal returned, smelling strongly of stables but looking well satisfied with the preparations he and Tim had made to take the horses to auction.

"What say the two of us go out for the evening?" he suggested after making himself presentable again.

Tara eagerly agreed. It had been much too long since they had spent any time alone together. "Is there transportation?"

"A car—of sorts," he said with a chuckle. "If we run out of gas, so much the better!"

An hour later Tara and Neal were headed down-hill in a vintage Morris. "Are you about finished exploring the island for handicrafts?" she asked.

"Oh, I could go on finding innovative stuff for months yet. Still, I don't want to overorder until I see how the merchandise sells at home."

Though he had evaded giving her a direct answer, Tara decided that the prospects of getting him back to the States soon sounded promising. It might just be wishful thinking, of course; a desire to see his trips with Eileen finished once and for all.

Neal knew of an inn at Longford which was justifiably famous for its good food. For a time, they ate and laughed like any other engaged couple who were very much in love. But Neal couldn't seem to keep his mind off his problems for very long.

"I wish I knew what arrangements Rory is making with the realtor," he said.

Tara frowned. "I don't understand why Kilgarrom wasn't left to Caithlin outright, so she could make her own decisions."

"Things are done differently here," Neal said flatly. "For hundreds of years Kilgarrom has been passed down in a direct line. Cormac had no son. By tradition, he was duty-bound to will the property to the oldest male relative."

"You? But—" Tara shifted uncomfortably in her chair. "Rory made it sound as though the two of you had inherited it together."

Neal's square jaw tightened. "I'm quite sure Cormac would have much preferred turning the place over to his younger nephew. However...be that as it may, we're both fond of Caithlin, and want to see her well provided for. In my view, there's only one way to ensure that."

Tara sighed. Selling Kilgarrom was the practical solution, she supposed. And yet.... "How does Rory feel about this decision?"

"It's only natural that he should resent allowing the property to go out of the family."

So his cousin was kicking up a fuss, Tara thought

perceptively. But she could tell from Neal's attitude that he had no intention of changing his mind. There were, he declared with a scowl, some papers he'd be insisting Rory sign—and the sooner the better!

Daylight had dwindled to a few pinkish rays on the horizon by the time they left the inn. Loathe to return just yet to Kilgarrom with its all too familiar problems, Neal proposed a visit to a nearby pub.

"I hope you're in good voice tonight," he joked. "More singing than drinking goes on in this place."

A line of napkin-sized tables huddled against the pub's back wall, but most of the patrons sat shoulder to shoulder on plain wooden benches. When they at last found a place to squeeze in, Tara saw that a small group of guitarists, most of whom seemed to be customers rather than professional entertainers, held the center of attention. Some of the songs they played were old, some new; they were tunes that every person present could, and did, sing.

"Slainte!" Neal raised his stein of Irish coffee in a toast.

All too soon the ten o'clock closing hour arrived. "I don't know when I've had such a wonderful time," Tara declared happily, walking back to the car with her fiancé's arm snuggled around her waist.

The low-hovering mist became a drizzle before they had driven many miles. But not even the weather could dampen her elation. She was still humming one of the lilting tunes from the pub when the elderly Morris chugged up the hill to Kilgarrom.

With both of them sheltering under Neal's rain-coat, they made a dash for the front entrance. He fished out an antique key, fumbling for the heavy lock. Inside, a lamp glowed on a table beneath Drucilla's portrait.

"You go on up." Sure that the older women of the household had already retired, he kissed her good night at the foot of the stairs. "I'll check around down here to make sure everything's in order."

Short as the distance across the courtyard had been, the penetrating dampness had soaked through Tara's shoes. A squishy squeak heralded every step she took. By the time she reached the upper hall, she had visions of puddles streaming out from the wet soles to mar the old carpet. Pausing at her bedroom door, she slipped out of the high heels.

It was then that she heard the voice, low and indistinct, from the foyer. Tara hesitated for a moment, then tiptoed back to peer down across the curving banister. Her lips parted to call to Neal, then closed again in silence. Eileen had just glided into view.

Eileen walked noiselessly across the foyer to lay a hand on Neal's arm. Her voice was muted; Tara couldn't distinguish a single word. But Neal seemed to have no difficulty understanding. His strong features took on a determined look. He slung the raincoat back across his shoulders.

Before he could move away, Eileen made an urgent gesture toward the still-burning lamp. Nodding agreement, Neal snuffed it out. Then they were through the door, two somber figures vanishing into the gloomy night.

CHAPTER FIVE

T ara didn't know which of them she was angrier at: Eileen for summoning him away, or Neal for going. But jealousy played little part in her ire. Common sense told her that what she had just witnessed was no romantic assignation. No. Something much less obvious was going on.

She still didn't like it. Not one bit. Neal was deliberately keeping secrets from her. If he'd do that during an engagement— Well, it made a poor basis for marriage, that was for sure!

Spinning around, she fled back to her room, determined to find out for herself what was taking place. A darting foray into the closet produced sturdy dry shoes and a navy-blue raincoat. As an afterthought she snatched up the waterproof hat to mask her bright hair.

45

Though she'd moved quickly, there was no sign of life in the courtyard when Tara slipped out the front door. She winced as the latch thudded into the jamb, then shrugged in resignation. Discovering what sort of dangerous escapade her fiancé was involved in was worth taking the risk of being locked out.

Because, quite suddenly, Tara felt convinced that it *was* dangerous. Eileen's urgency, the dark clothing she'd worn, her insistence that the light be extinguished—these things added up to cautious stealth.

It was raining steadily now. Moon and stars cowered behind scudding thunderheads. A hasty glance showed the old Morris standing wet and forlorn where Neal had parked it. Eileen's MG wasn't in sight, but Tara knew instinctively they hadn't taken that. She'd have heard the motor starting up.

Where, then, could they be? How could they have vanished so completely?

If their destination had been to the left, she reasoned, they'd have gone through the kitchen door. Therefore.... She turned toward the right-hand turret.

Her night vision improved, and with it her confidence. Tara strode purposefully across the cobblestones. Sorry now that she had not taken the opportunity to explore the grounds by daylight, she wondered what lay to the sides and rear of the castle.

As the red brick of the "modern" part of the structure gave way to the round roughness of ancient gray stone, her steps slowed. The turret belled out from the wall. The wide stone underfoot dwindled to a narrow path.

Still keeping to the shadows, she began to circle the turret. Suddenly, a powerful sense of danger intervened. Tara halted. She stared around, then down, and felt her throat constrict. Less than six feet away the level plateau on which the castle was built broke off. A black void yawned where she had presumed solid earth to be. Had she been running, and slipped—

Inching nearer the precipice, she saw that the incline was not particularly steep. Still, the slope tumbling down to a little inlet of Lough Duneen was rough and strewn with boulders and bushes.

A closer view told her that it was a landslide which had caused the earth to fall so abruptly away. How foolish, she thought, for Cormac or someone not to have protected the spot with a guardrail, at least!

She edged back onto the path, being extremely careful of her footing until the slide area was well to the rear and she had circled around behind the high, round turret. In the interval since she had left the house the rain had slackened. Light from a pale crescent of moon spread thinly over the ground.

It showed no trace of live people. Nothing but the tipsily leaning headstones of an old, old cemetery.

So exasperated she could have wept, Tara retraced her steps. People didn't simply vanish! Neal and Eileen must be somewhere close by.

It was as she stepped back from gravel to cobblestone that she heard the sound. Not loud enough to be called a noise, it was no more than a brief interruption of the night's deep silence. She stood very still, listening with all her might.

It came again. This time she had a name for it.

The sound that was not quite a noise was a squeak, coming from below. From the water. The squeak of oarlocks.

Tara caught her breath. Why, on a raw, windy night, should Neal and Eileen have descended some treacherous path to the lake, to board a rowboat? That they had done so seemed fairly evident. Because the squeak of oarlocks had just sounded again.

Anyone peering up from Lough Duneen at that moment would have noticed how determinedly straight across Tara's eyebrows looked, and at what a stubborn angle her chin tilted. She herself, scrambling down the least steeply slanted access to the drop, had no regard for appearances just then. All her concentration was riveted upon keeping her balance.

A third of the way down, a slick patch of leaves sent her skidding into a thorny bush. She landed hard, muttering a short epithet her older brothers were fond of saying at times such as this. Provoked at her own clumsiness, as well as at the other two for inciting this whole foolhardy chase, she tried bounding up and instead slithered all the way back in the mud.

It was fear that chased the anger away, fear bordering on panic as a huge shape loomed up beside her. Tara cringed aside, then almost giggled in relief.

"Gray Boy! Is that you?"

A cold nose touched her cheek.

"Come on, boy, help me up." She gripped a handful of shaggy, wet fur. "I guess we'd better try for a disorderly retreat."

She scooted through the mud and slick grass,

digging her heels in until she regained a sitting position. Then, using Gray Boy as a prop, she managed to plant both feet firmly on the ground and get herself turned around, heading back to the castle.

She groped for the wolfhound's collar. "Let's go, fellow!"

But Gray Boy wouldn't yield. He remained at rigid attention, long nose pointed downhill, tail arrow-stiff. Like a horizontal rocket, Tara thought, aiming at an unseen target.

It was to be her last thought for quite some time. A sudden Roman-candle burst of pain exploded in her head. She crumpled forward, collapsing onto the spongy earth.

A rock concert seemed to be going full blast inside her skull when consciousness came drifting back. Tara opened her eyes and saw Neal bending over her, frantic worry etching his features.

"Alannah! Are you all right?"

Before she could answer, footsteps tapped across the floor. Eileen's shamrock eyes were clouded with anxiety. "She's come 'round, has she?"

Neal nodded but did not look up. His eyes were still fixed on Tara's face. "See if you can sit up," he urged, helping her.

Woozily, she managed to do so. The throbbing in her head changed tempo. Tentatively she eased her fingers across the tennis-ball-sized lump at the base of her skull. A confused flash of memories pinwheeled back: the dog standing stock-still, the sudden pain, falling.

"Somebody hit me."

Even to her own ears, the announcement

sounded melodramatic. Not at all the proper thing to say while resting on a shabby couch next to the homely coziness of a coal stove in Kilgarrom's kitchen. Apparently Neal thought so too. He moved closer, cradling her hand in his. His lips brushed the damp feathers of hair clinging to her forehead.

"You fell, darlin'. There was a rock near where we found you. You slipped in the mud, and fell down and struck your head on it."

That was the sort of thing one said to a kindergartner, Tara reflected. A patient explanation in simple, one-syllable words, designed to make the hurt go away. And it wasn't true. Not a bit of it.

"Where's Gray Boy?" she demanded, playing for time while she tried to figure out why Neal seemed so eager for her to accept his so-pat explanation.

"In the pantry, gulping down ten pounds of dog food," Eileen answered.

"It's twenty he deserves," Neal claimed stoutly, "for leading us to you. He raised a terrible ruckus, prancing around down there, barking loud enough to raise the dead."

Tara let her eyelids flutter down. That wasn't true, either. Gray Boy hadn't barked. Or growled. Or even twitched. He'd just stood there, planted in the footpath like an oak tree, and stared down the hill. Someone—two someones, probably—had come up from the lake. People Gray Boy knew. There'd been no ruckus, not a whimper of warning, when one of those someones got close enough to strike her down.

Icy fingers touched her heart. But it couldn't have been Neal. He loved her! He wouldn't—

Her eyes opened to fasten pleadingly on her fiancé. "Neal, where did you go? I was still in the corridor upstairs when you and Eileen left the house tonight. It looked as though something might be amiss, so I got my coat and followed you. Or tried to. You weren't . . . anywhere."

He turned slightly, reaching for the steaming cup Eileen had just filled from the kettle. "Sip this, Tara. It'll do you good."

She didn't want the tea but took it anyway, conscious suddenly of her scratched hands and the mud caked under her nails. What a sight she must look!

Neal waited until she had swallowed a mouthful of the warming brew. "We went around back, sweetheart. That's why you didn't see us. Earlier, Eileen had heard some peculiar noises outside. As soon as we came home she asked me to take a look around. It's lonely here, and she was feeling a trifle nervous."

Tara cast her mind back to the scene in the foyer. If that was a sample of Eileen's nervousness, the girl ought to take up test-piloting.

She glanced over at Eileen. "Was it oarlocks you heard?"

The room became very still. Eileen's pot holdered hand tightened around the kettle, and Neal had the look of Gray Boy, untwitchingly stiff on the slope of the hill.

"Oarlocks?" Eileen repeated numbly.

"Yes. You know—on a rowboat. When you pull back on the oars the boat moves through the water, and the hinge the oar is locked into makes a noise. It squeaks." Now *she* sounded like the kindergarten teacher, Tara thought in disgust. "I heard them. That's why I tried climbing down the hill."

"Poachers!" Neal snapped his fingers. "That accounts for your peculiar noises too, Eileen. They must have been snaring game in the woods, and they took to their heels when we came out. No doubt they came by boat and left the same way."

Eileen came to life again. She set the kettle back on the range and picked up the broom, sweeping away the clods of mud their shoes had tracked in. "You're right, of course," she agreed, poker-faced. "I certainly hope they won't be back. It would be best if we didn't mention this to Caithlin and Brigid. They get into a terrible dither at the idea of prowlers."

"None of us will say a word." Neal plucked the cup from Tara's fingers and lifted her off the couch as if she had been a rag doll. Throwing a caution over his shoulder about banking the stove, he headed up the back stairs.

"Better wash the grime off your pretty face and get some rest," he said, setting her down in the doorway of her room.

Tara's arms tightened around his neck. "Neal— are you sure it was just poachers?"

"Who else could it have been, *alannah?*"

Who else indeed, she wondered later, tossing and turning in the four-poster bed. Poachers were almost the perfect answer to everything that had happened that night. Except that Neal and Eileen *hadn't* been "around back." The moon, anemic as it was, would have revealed their presence. And she *hadn't* knocked herself unconscious by slipping and hitting her head on a rock. And Gray Boy *hadn't* barked.

Neal's explanation was blarney from start to finish!

CHAPTER SIX

T he bump on Tara's head was still extremely tender the next morning. Other sections of her anatomy ached too. She found that by concentrating very hard on the assortment of scrapes and bruises she'd collected it was possible to forget less tangible hurts like worries and doubts and suspicions for whole minutes at a time.

From halfway down the stairs she could hear Molly singing in the kitchen. When Tara joined her, the hired girl brought a steaming dish of porridge to the table, then pulled a folded square of paper from her apron pocket.

"Mr. Neal left this letter for you," she said. "He rode off an hour ago, with that Tim from the stables, and declared I was to give it to you first thing."

Some of the numbing uncertainty of the previous night came rushing back as Tara accepted the little sheet of lined paper Molly handed her. Had Neal changed his mind, and decided to tell her what had really happened down by the lake? Or would this message have something to do with Eileen?

Becoming aware of the friendly curiosity Molly was exuding, Tara flipped open the note. Her face fell. The few lines in Neal's familiar scrawl concerned nothing momentous, after all. Due to all the rain and the boggy state of some of the roads they'd be traveling over, he said, the stableman was anxious to begin moving the horses to Athlone at once. They couldn't afford to delay, since the next auction would not take place for two or three months. Therefore, he had no choice but to help Tim transfer the stock to the fairgrounds.

He added a postscript: *Will return Sunday. Don't let Rory go back to Dublin until I've had a talk with him. Very important!*

There was a funny squiggle at the end which could have said "love," followed by an almost unreadable initial. Tara scanned it a second time, telling herself it was foolish to expect valentine verses in a hastily penned note, then set it aside. It was hard not to wonder whether hurrying off to Athlone had been Neal's own idea. Maybe he was hoping that by Sunday she would have forgotten about things like squeaky oarlocks and rocks that jumped up and smacked innocent people on the head.

Moping about it wasn't going to help. At least, she thought, with an un-Tara-like flicker of cattiness, Eileen would have to attend to her own "peculiar noises" for the next few nights.

Instantly she dismissed the notion as unfair. Eileen might or might not be a beautiful manhunter, but she wasn't a scaredy-cat. Or a shirker, either. Long past midnight she'd been busy, building a fire, making tea, sweeping the floor.

Not sweeping it very well, however. There were still traces of mud on the well-worn linoleum. Spying them, she remembered Eileen's casual-sounding remark about not mentioning the escapade to Caithlin and Brigid. On reflection, Tara decided that their nervousness about prowlers was not what Eileen had had in mind at all. The secret she and Neal shared was being kept from the other women too. And muddy footprints would have raised too many questions.

Tara shoved back her chair, tied an apron around her waist, and grabbed the broom. She didn't want any questions, either. Not until she herself knew the answers!

Helping to get the house ready for company, Tara learned that there were at least twenty rooms on the ground floor. All were vast and high-ceilinged, with faded brocade draperies and rugs worn to pale wraiths of their once-rich colors.

Tara tried to visualize a family clustered around a snapping fire in one of the wide stone hearths, but soon abandoned the attempt. No place this big could ever have been cozy, even with plenty of furniture to fill the spaces. Now hardly enough of it remained to counteract the echoes. Whitish squares on the yellowed walls testified to pictures having been removed, one by one. Sold in hard times like the furniture, she supposed.

She did her best to create at least the impression of a lived-in look, all the time marveling that anyone with fewer than a score of children would have wanted so much space. At lunchtime she expressed this thought to Caithlin, who smiled and said that in years gone by, people did have enormous families.

"Besides, Drucilla wanted her home to be as magnificent as any palace in England."

"Keeping up with the Tudors!"

"With her father's family, at least. At any rate, she completely remodeled Kilgarrom. The keep, where the foyer and staircase and a few surrounding rooms on both floors now stand, was the castle's original living quarters. It must have been a damp, crowded place in those days. Drucilla had the builders fill the whole expanse with rooms."

The third floor was still unfinished at the time of Kevin Fitzgarth's death. It had never been used as anything but an attic. "Lots of old junk up there," Caithlin said, summing up the accumulation of the centuries.

Tara inquired about the passageway that Drucilla and her twin sons had used to make their escape from her father's wrath. Unfortunately, Caithlin was able to tell her nothing about it.

"Could have been just a romantic fillip to the old tale. Or mayhap it was boarded up later, after the landslide. Who knows?"

There was too much work to be done to sit any longer, gossiping about the past. Eileen pitched in and helped Tara scrub and polish and sparkle up the downstairs windows in preparation for the spiritualists' visit. On the second floor Caithlin opened one rosewood chest after another, hauling out fragrant, age-yellowed linens for Brigid and Molly to spread on the beds.

"Cormac was right in forbidding them to come

here," Eileen grumbled. "He'd have asked Caithlin how she expected a gaggle of the hated English to pacify her blasted Lady with the Harp."

"It's only for one night." Tara paused in her dusting. "Are the British still so disliked here?"

An odd expression flickered in Eileen's eyes. "By some. Old feuds die hard."

She would probably be even stiffer tomorrow, Tara realized. But the improved appearance of the house was worth a few aching muscles. With the dust sheets removed and the tangy scent of furniture polish replacing the moldy odor of mildew, the old rooms seemed to have mellowed into a new loveliness.

In midafternoon Eileen and Caithlin drove off to Ballycroom to buy groceries for the buffet dinner. Feeling grubby from all the exertion, Tara decided to indulge in the luxury of a bath and shampoo in the middle of the day.

During the short time she had been at Kilgarrom, the climate had fluctuated constantly, from mist to drizzle to drenching rain, and now to glorious sunshine. Strolling outside to dry her hair in the warm air, she marveled at how entirely different daylight made everything seem. The castle didn't appear a bit eerie now, with the bright, golden rays sparkling against the red and gray surfaces of its walls and turrets.

She wondered how it had looked in Drucilla's day. For some reason, the Lady with the Harp refused to leave her thoughts. Though that was preferable to dwelling on Neal's unaccountable behavior, Tara felt rather sheepish in admitting the fact. Soon she'd be as obsessed as Caithlin! But it wasn't the same thing at all. In her case, curiosity could be classed as professional interest. As a genealogist, she couldn't ignore the very distinct probability that her family and Drucilla's had once been closely related.

At the moment, however, the likeness between their two faces was all she had to go on. Suddenly, she remembered the graveyard at the rear of the castle. There was a slim chance that if it had been Drucilla's last resting place, her maiden name might be chiseled on a tombstone. She hurried around the gravel path to the unkempt patch of hallowed ground. The drooping picket fence surrounding it was almost as dilapidated as the markers themselves. Carefully, she swung open the gate and stepped inside.

Cemeteries held no terror for her. She had poked through many a burying place in search of a clue to someone's ancestry. Now she bent to inspect the half-toppled headstones. The two nearest the gate apparently marked the graves of the last persons to be laid to rest here. Both granite stones showed the year of death as 1916. The date sparked an echo in Tara's history-conscious mind. Cormac Fitzgarth's parents had died in that year, a bare six weeks apart.

The headstone she sought would not be nearly so recent. She moved from mound to mound, peering at dates, finding them sometimes almost obliterated by wind and weather, until she reached the last row. There she saw it, lying on its side, but with the deeply etched letters still legible.

DRUCILLA
Sorrowing wife of Kevin Fitzgarth
June 14, 1702—March 10, 1781

Tara could have gritted her teeth in frustration. Not so much as an initial to indicate whom she had been before marrying Kevin! The birthday might help, though. She committed it to memory, hoping that by tracing back old records of her mother's ascendants, she might find a daughter named Drucilla born to one of them on that date.

So the search had not been a total loss. She had one more clue to the identity of her look-alike. But it would still be a formidable task to trace a connection between the two families.

A chord of apprehension clouded the bright day. Would those two families ever be united? Less than twenty-four hours ago she and Neal had been happily discussing plans for their future. It had seemed then that they were meant for each other. Now his secretiveness about the midnight venture with Eileen had spread a blight on her carefree certainty. Could she marry a man who skimped on the truth?

Tara's face was downcast as she closed the gate on the neglected graveyard and started back along the gravel path. To her right lay the broken edge of the hill. She slowed, wondering how she had found the courage to plunge down that precipice in the rain.

On impulse, she moved nearer the brink. It wasn't dark or rainy now. The broad expanse of Lough Duneen appeared calm enough to be immobile, as though some giant hand had flung the water across an ironing board and pressed it into a starched blue tablecloth.

Neal had said that the poachers came by boat and departed in the same way. Tara ached to believe him, to shed the oppressive burden of doubt. An idea of how he might be proven right popped into her head. If there really had been poachers trespassing on the premises, no boat would be moored at the bottom of the slope. They would have paddled away in it!

It wouldn't be hard, now, to climb down and see. Make sure.

She hesitated, afraid all at once to take the step. Wouldn't it be better to ignore her doubts and simply accept Neal's word?

Tara was in the midst of a heated debate with herself when she saw the head. That's all it was at first, just the head of a man bobbing around far below. She caught her breath, then felt slightly ridiculous as the rest of him came into view, an inch or two of speckled tweed at a time. A flattish cap was angled jauntily on his head. In his hand swung a gnarled walking stick. It darted out ahead of him like a third leg, helping him maintain his footing on the slick surface of the incline.

She strode a few yards along the path, ready to intercept him when he reached the top. Seen close, he looked older than she had thought at first. Fifty, perhaps. There was a ruggedness about his clothes and shoulders and craggy face that gave the impression of an ordinary country man. Yet when he turned keen blue eyes on her, the notion was quickly erased.

"This is private property," she said in a politely firm tone. "If you are lost, I can direct you to the road."

"That won't be necessary. My name is Thomas Sheridan, miss. Inspector Sheridan."

Tara's level brows arched in surprise. "A policeman? I don't understand. Did you come by boat?"

"I did not." He stared sternly down at her. Tara

knew for a certainty that if she'd been guilty of any lawbreaking, those penetrating, deep-set eyes would have torn a confession out of her without another word being spoken.

"The *gardai* at Ballycroom reported sighting a boat headed 'round this way late last evening." His announcement sounded weighty with import.

She blinked. "What's a *gardai?*"

"One policeman. Two would be *garda*. Since there is only one in Ballycroom. . . ."

A feeling of intense relief flooded Tara's heart. Neal had been truthful with her, after all. Like an idiot, she'd doubted his word! She glanced back at Inspector Sheridan. "That doesn't explain what you're doing here now. Were they breaking the curfew, or something?"

Apparently he had been expecting a different reaction. "We've no curfew in the Republic," he said shortly. "If we had, it would be no responsibility of mine to enforce it. It is my duty to ask what the people in this house were doing last night. You'd be an American, wouldn't you, now?"

"I would," she snapped, unconsciously adopting the Irish form of speech. Was he accusing her and Neal of something merely because they were foreigners?

"My name is Tara Delevan. I am engaged to be married to Neal Riordan, Mrs. Fitzgarth's nephew. My fiancé and I spent last evening in Longford. We returned a little before midnight. The older ladies were asleep, but Eileen O'Keefe, a friend of the family, came to meet us saying that she had heard noises. The three of us went outside to investigate, but saw nothing. I slipped and fell partway down this hill. My fiancé carried me back to the house. After having a cup of tea, we all went to bed."

Out of breath, Tara conquered the urge to add "So there!" to the terse but truthful recital. She hadn't told a lie, not one, and he needn't think that any amount of staring at her was going to do him any good.

But his belligerence seemed to have disintegrated under the cascade of words. "Ah! I wondered about the trampled marks in the mud down there," he observed blandly. "Lucky you didn't hurt yourself when you fell. I suppose you were too well occupied to notice a boat, or anything out of the ordinary?"

"It was dark. Raining. There could have been one, I guess. Neal suspected that it might have been poachers Eileen heard."

"Poachers? How...convenient. In that case I've just been wasting my time." He tipped his cap, revealing a freckled pate with just a fringe of grayish hair curving around it, like a smile on backward.

Annoyed, Tara called him back when he turned and started walking toward the driveway. "Wait a minute! Aren't you going to tell me what this is all about?"

"Just checking up." He paused to stare back at her. "That's only natural, wouldn't you think, considering how Cormac Fitzgarth met his end?"

"He drowned. Didn't he?"

The inspector nodded. "Oh, yes. He drowned. So did the four men who were with him in the boat, after they were stunned by the explosion." The blue eyes raked across her face. "Lough Duneen connects with a whole series of lakes, didn't you know? There's a clear waterway straight into Ulster. Cormac and his group used that route to smuggle guns and ammunition into the north counties. The last time, the border police caught them at it. They tried to get away, and— Well, it only took one bullet to blow up the boat."

"You aren't serious!"

"Certainly I am. You'll read in the newspaper that this war in the six counties is a religious fight, Catholic against Protestant. Cormac didn't give a rap about which pulpit the Sunday sermon was preached from. He was in it to do down the British."

Eileen's words drifted back to her. "Old feuds die hard." So this was what she had meant!

"Even today you'll see 'Sinn Féin' chalked on walls, and hear of people who've long since gone off to America joining the IRA—the Irish Republican Army," Inspector Sheridan added, watching her closely.

Tara wouldn't have believed it was possible to feel so cold on such a sunny day. She forced a question out through dry, stiff lips: "If Cormac and his companions drowned, why are you still so interested in boats?"

"Sure, miss," he said, leaning on his walking stick for just a moment longer, "I didn't say all his friends had drowned!"

CHAPTER SEVEN

"There is a definite aura here," Mrs. Addison-Heap proclaimed. Her long nose quivered receptively as she passed the closed door at the head of the stairs. "I can feel it!"

Tara was helping to escort the members of the Spiritualist Society to their rooms. She mustered what she hoped was a neutral smile. "Can you? It's an interesting old house, with a very long history. I hope you'll be comfortable during your stay."

The men of the party seemed to be as enthusiastic as the women. Words like "ectoplasm" and "manifestation" echoed along the corridor. Farther down Tara could hear Eileen explaining the origin of the crystal chandeliers and discreetly indicating the location of the bathrooms.

"Whist! What a shock they'll get when they find

67

out there are only two," Molly giggled, scampering down the back steps ahead of Tara.

For the first time all day the kitchen was empty. Brigid had shut herself in her room, flatly refusing to honor what she called "heathen rites" with her presence. Caithlin stood in the foyer bidding a rather tentative welcome to her guests as they straggled in.

A full twenty-four hours had passed since that unsettling encounter on the hillside. At the beginning, Tara was too shaken to discuss Inspector Sheridan's visit with anyone. Besides, in whom could she confide? It was unthinkable that she should resurrect old sorrows by mentioning the man's allegations to Caithlin. And she couldn't talk to Brigid. The elderly housekeeper was already convinced that Tara was destined to bring calamity to Kilgarrom. Policemen poking around would only solidify that notion.

Her reasons for avoiding Eileen were not so simple to analyze. They were there, though, at the back of her head. Jealousy played a surprisingly small part in them. When finally she had gone to bed, she'd lain awake for hours, hearing the inspector's last words over and over again. Wondering. Trying to pry apart the innuendoes and winnow out the real meaning underneath.

"Molly," she said now, thankful that for once the girl had agreed to stay late, "what does *Sinn Féin* mean?" She pronounced it *shin fayn* as the policeman had done.

Molly's darting-quick response showed that she understood the Gaelic phrase perfectly. "Where did you hear that?"

"Someone mentioned seeing it chalked on a wall."

"Ah, schoolboys, no doubt. Those little devils would write anything." She swooped over to the ice chest, and backed out again with two heaping salad bowls in her hands. "'Tis an old slogan meaning 'ourselves alone.' It used to be very popular during the Troubles, I'm told."

"'Ourselves alone'? That's an odd sort of slogan."

Molly shrugged, nearly tipping a quantity of potato salad onto the floor. "Battle cry, then. Ourselves, the Irish; alone—without the English." Her orange-red mop of hair flying out behind her, Molly vanished through the dining-room door.

Not quite up to "Give me liberty or give me death," but along the same lines. Tara sighed. She might have known. Along with the talk of smuggled weapons, it was just another hint of the intrigue that seemed designed to keep the island in a turmoil. Worrisome. But not so worrisome as the implications in the inspector's words about Americans joining the IRA. He couldn't have been talking about Neal, could he?

Hearing voices in the main part of the house, she hurried to set out the platters of meat. Tara was filling the sugar bowl and preparing the coffee service for Molly to carry in when Eileen entered the kitchen.

"Aren't you joining us?"

"I'd really rather not." Tara handed a tray of cups and saucers to Molly, and waited until the girl had crossed into the next room. "There were several comments upstairs on my resemblance to Drucilla. One man was ranting on about reincarnation.

I'd prefer to have them concentrate on the original model."

Eileen groaned. "How I wish this night were over! As soon as they finish eating, the men intend to set up a circle of chairs in the foyer, directly beneath the portrait."

"Seems like a pretty drafty place to hold a seance. Do they expect raps on the table, or what?"

"Who knows?" Amusement flickered, ruffling Eileen's usual mask of polite aloofness. "Why don't we watch from the hall? Caithlin can stay with us. I don't believe she's very keen on becoming part of the group."

Tara admitted that she was curious as to what would take place. "Maybe I'll be along later," she half promised.

No more was said because Molly returned to the kitchen just then. "Bunch of sillies in there, with all that talk of clairvoyants and mediums and life on another plane," she sniffed. "Oh, miss, you don't suppose they're a witch's coven, do you?"

"Nothing like that," Tara assured her. "These people just believe that some spirits remain close to earth for a time after death, instead of going straight to heaven."

"Skipping purgatory, I suppose, and ignoring hell altogether?"

"I wouldn't know about that. They really are sincere, though. Spiritualists try to contact the departed through mediums—people whose voices are used to carry messages from the dead back here to the living."

Molly declared that it sounded positively unchristian to her. She continued to look so uneasy that Tara herself took over the task of clearing the dishes from the dining room.

With the two of them working together, putting the kitchen to rights did not take long. The chore couldn't be finished too quickly for Molly. The suds were still whisking down the drain when she flapped a scarf over her head and departed for Ballycroom on her bicycle.

Her desertion left Tara with no excuse for not joining the others. Very quietly, she walked past the dimly lit rooms to the center of the house. The corridor itself lay in deep shadow; no chandeliers burned along its length tonight.

She halted just in time to avoid colliding with Eileen. "Have I missed anything exciting?"

"Not a thing." Eileen sounded bored. "They've been holding hands and meditating, but so far nobody's gone into a trance. Perhaps the aura here is the wrong color."

Caithlin spoke from a chair that had been placed for her near the edge of the entrance hall. She looked dignified and sad in her widow's garb. "It's sorry I am that you've all been subjected to this. If anyone's spirit returned tonight it would be himself's, telling me what a daft old fool I was to encourage these misguided folk."

Tara reached down to squeeze her hand. Peering over Caithlin's shoulder, she saw that a single candle burned on the table around which the group sat. More shadows than light seemed to emanate from its flickering flame. The faces of those present could scarcely be distinguished, let alone the portrait high on the wall. Yet there could be no doubt that Drucilla was the focus of attention here. Tara herself could picture the scene that had taken place on this very spot two and a half centuries earlier: The massive entrance doors bursting open; Kevin Fitzgarth's life blood spilling across the tile; his bride, horrified, helpless upon the stairway—

She clenched her fists and half turned, trying to blot out the vision. The entire area was emotion-charged, vibrating with some intense passion. It was too much! None of it was real, yet she was caught in the midst of it. Neal's family or not, she had to get away from Kilgarrom, and soon!

Then it happened. Suddenly, without warning. In the throb of one heartbeat the candle guttered and winked out. From somewhere far above a single note wafted forth, then another, and a third. Lyrical notes, strummed on a harp. An old, old melody, tinkling through the electrified air.

She wanted to move, to run away, but the chords held her spellbound. Caithlin's hand was like cold, rigid marble in her own. The music of the harp strings rose and fell. Echoed away. Back into the past, it seemed, whence it had come.

It was Eileen who recovered her senses first. Spinning around, she darted into the nearest parlor and returned with a lamp. She raised it high at the edge of the foyer, letting the bright rays beam out across the assembled group. Every man and woman sat as they had sat before. Immobilized. Rapt.

None of them, Tara knew with utter certainty, had been responsible for what had taken place. The eerie, haunting tune had descended on them from above. Even if one had wished to trick the others, no human being could have run so swiftly and silently up that high, curving staircase and down again.

The candle was speedily relit, by which time Tara had caught her own breath. Only thirty or forty seconds had drummed by since the last note sang out. Not time enough for an intruder lurking above to make his escape.

"Bring the lamp. Let's see what's up there," she hissed to Eileen.

Their footsteps clicked rapidly across the floor, up the tattered runner. The door at the head of the stairs stood ajar, the first time Tara had ever seen it thus.

"Whose room is that?"

"Can't you guess?" Within the glossy black frame of hair, Eileen's face looked deathly pale. "It's the master bedchamber, but no one has used it in nearly two centuries. The furniture—everything—is just the way Drucilla left it."

"Where does Brigid sleep?"

"At the end of the corridor, next to Caithlin's bathroom." The lamp trembled in Eileen's hand. "You aren't thinking that she...."

"She's the only one up here, isn't she? Molly went home. I bolted the door behind her myself. And you saw everyone downstairs." Tara was already on her way down the hall. "They were all too paralyzed to move. So who played the harp?"

Not Brigid, she realized immediately. Moonlight streamed across the housekeeper's bed, outlining the wizened figure asleep there. Deep, even breaths that were almost snores droned sonorously from the top of the quilts. Tara backed out of the room, her theory deflated.

Eileen added another puncture to it. "She's half crippled with arthritis. Haven't you noticed how gnarled her hands are? Brigid couldn't coax music out of a harp even if she wanted to scare us all witless. Besides, she is too devoted to Caithlin to do such a thing."

Tara turned to stare at her. Her voice sank to a whisper. "Who would, then?"

No answer was forthcoming. More frightened than she cared to admit, Tara took the lamp from Eileen's now badly shaking hand and returned to the head of the stairs. There was nothing inviting about that half-open door, and it was a moment before she could steel her courage to step inside.

Here the moonlight seemed more diffused, mistier. The room was cold as a crypt. It was quite evident that no human form had lain on the grandly canopied bed in a very long time. The satin covering was blanketed with dust, and the overhanging draperies looked as if they would disintegrate at the first stirring of air.

Tara fancied that she could hear her heart thudding as she moved across the Persian carpet. On the wall opposite the bed stood a huge waist-high marriage chest. The chest itself was so richly carved that no ornament was needed to accentuate its beauty, yet one object rested on the wood-grained surface.

A small, gilt Irish harp.

Advancing toward it, she raised the lamp. All around its base the dust lay thick and even. She bent lower, puffing a breath across the silent strings. A cloud of dust drifted upward.

"Well?" Eileen asked from the doorway.

Tara shook her head. "It hasn't been touched. Not—not for centuries."

* * *

Rory arrived the next morning, soon after the house party had dispersed. Tara saw his blue Rover screech across the courtyard and stop with a burst of gravel near the kitchen door. He unfolded his long body from the cramped seat with a series of jerks, slammed the car door violently, and stalked up the path. He looked to be in even more of a towering rage than the first time she had met him. A moment later he came banging into the room and thudded a carton of groceries onto the table.

Peeking inside it, Tara saw two plump chickens, a round of cheese, and some fruit. "You're a kind-hearted fellow, Rory McDermott, in spite of your surly disposition," she teased, trying to coax him out of his black mood. "What have you been doing —collecting more uninvited travelers from Shannon?"

"Nothing quite so dreadful as that." The corners of his mouth began to quirk up. "Just a breakdown on the road. Carburetor trouble. It forced me to stop over in Longford, otherwise I'd have been here last night."

"Cead mile fáilte to you, anyway. Have you had your breakfast?"

"I have." He tossed his wrinkled coat over a chair and gave her a roguish smile. "Why is it that you are here, still, and not off on a honeymoon with my cousin?"

"What, and take all those horses with us? We'll wait until we can enjoy our privacy, thank you."

Tara parried Rory's thrust with unconcern, better prepared this time for his irksome manner. She had no intention of allowing him to get the upper hand again. Explaining that Neal and the stableman were attending a livestock auction in Athlone, she busied herself by storing away the food he had brought.

"Neal left a message for you," she added. "Please don't go back to Dublin until he has had a chance to talk with you. I know he's anxious to discuss putting Kilgarrom up for sale."

"Always in a rush, these Americans." When that statement failed to provoke a flash of temper from Tara, Rory grinned and promised not to disappoint Neal. "Come out and take a stroll with me in the fresh air," he said. "I need a breath to clear the fumes of that wretched car from my head. And why should I walk alone when there's a pretty girl to keep me company?"

"No reason at all, providing you behave yourself."

As a matter of fact, Tara was glad of the excuse to get outside. Since the previous evening the atmosphere within the house seemed to have been growing more and more oppressive.

Beside her, Rory tramped along in companionable silence. "Do you like Ireland?" he asked presently.

"Indeed I do. But I'm finding it a bit bewildering." Tara paused and looked up at him. "Rory, why didn't you tell me about Cormac? About the way he died?"

One black eyebrow shot up, questioningly. "What, and rattle the skeletons in the cupboard? Who's been talking out of turn to you?"

"A man named Inspector Sheridan. I found him poking around the hillside Thursday afternoon." Tara dropped down on a boulder. "He said that

Cormac had smuggled guns to the insurgents up north. His story sounded pretty convincing."

Rory propped his lean back against a tree. "Oh, it's true enough. I never did hear how they were found out." He scowled. "You didn't mention this to Caithlin, I hope."

"Of course not, nor to anyone else until now. Neal had left that morning, and—and it wouldn't have been kind to upset the others. But it's all terribly confusing. The inspector said Cormac was in the plot because he hated the English. Ireland has been free for years now. Why would he continue such a horrible vendetta?"

"It's only Eire—the Republic—that's free. The six counties of Northern Ireland are still under British rule," Rory reminded her. "To be fair, the majority of people up there voted to keep it that way. But Cormac— His father was slain by the Black and Tans, a cruel special force of British police, in the Easter Rebellion. He was just a lad then. His mother died soon afterward, and during the Troubles he and his little sisters nearly followed their parents into the grave. My own mother used to tell stories about those terrible days. It was only Cormac's quick-wittedness that kept them all alive."

"That was a long time ago; 1916, wasn't it?" Tara was remembering the dates on the tombstones.

"A long time to let the hatred fester," Rory agreed. "What were the *garda* doing here, anyway?"

"Inspector Sheridan came alone," Tara said absently. "The Ballycroom police reported sighting a boat headed in this direction the night before. And though I didn't admit it to him, I'm certain a boat did come right up to the base of the hill."

That startled Rory. "What makes you think so?"

"I heard it." Talking about that night, when oar-locks had pierced through wind and rain with their squeak, she remembered standing alone at the edge of the precipice. Listening. Wondering where Neal and Eileen had disappeared to. She still hadn't learned the truth about where they had gone. Somewhere close by, yet out of sight.

She glanced up suddenly. "Rory, those old tur-rets at each end of the castle—can they be entered from the courtyard?"

"They can, if one knows which stone to push." He gave her a baffled look. "Are you crediting the boatmen with nerve enough to break into the house?"

Tara hopped off the boulder. "Nothing like that. But this is my first experience with castles. Could you show me what the inside of a turret looks like?"

"The one on this end is still safe enough to enter," he said, after a moment's consideration. "I used to play knights and dragons there when I was a lad. You'll find it a dank, crowded place, though, I warn you."

Rory took her arm protectively as they strolled back toward the house. The interior of the turret nearest the cliff had been demolished before the turn of the century, he said, when the landslide rat-tled Kilgarrom's foundations. It was a wonder the whole thing hadn't collapsed completely.

Excitement bubbled within Tara when Rory led her up the rugged stone tower. "Open it," he chal-lenged her.

After pressing and thumping and prying at each block within her reach, she laughingly admitted failure. "Any medieval dragon would have enjoyed a nice barbecue meal of me!"

"Um—tasty thought."

With a motion that was both twist and thrust, Rory manipulated an all-but-invisible catch concealed in the crevice between two of the huge gray stones. A three-foot-high section of the turret protestingly creaked open.

Tara bent and followed him inside. She straightened up next to a winding staircase whose narrow, uneven footholds appeared to have been chipped from a single massive boulder. The steps spiraled up and up, dwindling out of sight as she craned to see the top.

"Why, it's like a lighthouse! But there isn't much room down here."

"Of course not. Do you think the builders wanted to leave space for the dragons to chase them inside?"

Rory's face sobered then. He shrugged aside childhood's fancies. The turrets had served as lookout towers, he said. When an enemy approached, archers could rain arrows down through the thin vertical slits in the walls while they themselves remained well protected. And should, by some dire chance, the foe manage to break in, the steps had been set in a clockwise spiral. This left room on the right for the defenders' sword-arms, and put the attackers at a disadvantage.

A latticework of cobwebs trailed across the steps; dust carpeted the stone flooring. The gap between stairway and wall was a curving arc about six feet wide. Surveying it with her eye, Tara realized that she was no closer than before to solving the riddle of where Neal and Eileen had gone that night. Even if they knew about this secret entrance, why should they have hidden here?

The penetrating dampness inside the tower was beginning to chill her bones. Tara shivered and ducked back outside.

Rory shoved the doorway into place again. "Pity you'll never have the chance to play damsel in distress here," he commented. "Neal seems determined to sell Kilgarrom."

"Oh, I know how you must feel." Sympathetically Tara turned to face him. "But don't you see? It's for Caithlin's sake he is doing it. She can't go on living here. Even if it weren't ten times too big for her, this constant preoccupation with ghosts isn't healthy. She nearly collapsed last night after the seance."

Signs of an imminent thundercloud flitted across Rory's face. "*What* seance?"

Briefly, she told him about the visit of the Spiritualist Society, and the weird aftermath of their convocation.

"Hearing that harp music—it was just plain eerie. Maybe...maybe Drucilla *is* still roaming Kilgarrom." Tara's eyes grew wide and fearful. "I don't know *what* to believe anymore!"

CHAPTER EIGHT

L eaning out her window with a welcome for the sparkling Sunday that had dawned not long before, Tara caught sight of a lean, hip-booted figure ambling down the slope toward Lough Duneen. A fishing rod was slung carelessly over Rory's shoulder; a creel flapped at his side. Proper heathen he was, she thought, drawing back inside to dress for church.

Eileen echoed this opinion less tolerantly when, an hour later, he had not returned. "I suppose we can all fit in my car if we hold our breath," she said. "You first, Caithlin, then Brigid. Thank heaven we're all slim. Can you squeeze in on the edge, Tara?"

Most of Ballycroom seemed to be heading in the same direction. Children masked impish grins behind best-behavior primness. Behind them, the women emerging from the thatch-roofed cottages were dressed in the brightest colors imaginable. At the door of the church they separated from their menfolk to sit on opposite sides of the aisle from them. It made for a peacock and sparrow sort of congregation, Tara reflected: rainbow hues of crimson and orange and green on the left; somber gray tweed on the right.

In a way, the church was much like its parishioners. Vivid stained-glass windows provided a glittering contrast to the dull, slate-colored stone from which St. Brendan's was built. There were eight of them, high and arched, painstakingly fashioned. Scrollwork letters in the lower corner of each window memorialized the donating family: *O'Reilly, Fitzgarth, Sullivan, Mullins....*

Tara's conscience gave an uncomfortable twinge. Annie Mullins and her mother had already confirmed that the Ballycroom Ardells were not part of the family she had been commissioned to trace. So what was she waiting for? Why nearly a week spent at Kilgarrom, when she should have been in Dublin, sifting through pertinent records?

Tomorrow, she told herself. *I'll leave tomorrow. Neal can take me. If we can both get away from here quickly....*

There was relief in having made a firm decision. Whatever was going on at Kilgarrom was none of her business. Or Neal's. It was...better that they leave. For some reason her mind provided the word "safer." Tara pushed the unwelcome notion away. Better, that was all. Better for everyone.

And the Ardill family tree provided the best excuse in the world to leave.

Afterward, while her companions walked back to

the quiet little cemetery to visit Cormac's grave, Tara paused on the church steps for a word with the pastor.

"Genealogy, is it?" Father O'Dea asked, taking an immediate interest. "You're welcome to look through my books, if you like. Everyone who's been baptized or married or buried from St. Brendan's since 1804 is listed there. Only the village folk, mind. If the family you're seeking wasn't from Ballycroom, you'd do well to start your search at Dublin Castle."

"Yes, I had planned to." Tara was aware that the building he had named was the Republic's foremost record depository. "I'm not sure which county the ancestor of my client came from."

Tara thanked him and walked back to the car. It was disappointing that the local church records didn't extend a few years further back. Had they spanned another quarter century, they might have been of help in searching out Drucilla's background.

She sighed impatiently. She was beginning to wish she had never heard of Drucilla Fitzgarth!

Something about the affair of the Lady with the Harp kept bothering her. The notion had been playing hide-and-seek with the back of Tara's mind ever since the seance. There was something, some question, she knew she ought to ask Caithlin. The answer might help clear up part of this enigma. But she couldn't quite put her finger on what it was. The harder she pondered, the more elusive the idea became.

She turned to catch sight of the others approaching. Even had she managed to identify the troublesome detail that kept sliding away from her, Tara wouldn't have had the heart to put it to Caithlin just then. Lines of strain marred the older woman's face as she walked slowly back from a visit to her husband's grave. She looked ill, used up, as though recent events had been almost more than she could endure.

Fortunately, the return trip to Kilgarrom took only a few minutes. Tara lingered beside the car until Brigid had hustled her mistress inside. Then she turned to Eileen with a concerned frown. "I don't believe Caithlin is at all well."

"She may well have caught a chill, sitting in that draft the other night. I've already suggested having Dr. Findlay pay a call. But she simply won't listen to me and allow him to come."

Tara hesitated, feeling helpless. "Well, keep an eye on her, anyway. I plan to leave for Dublin tomorrow, and. . . ."

Eileen thrust the car into gear. "Don't you be worrying. We take good care of our own here."

Tara could have sworn that a spark of elation glimmered in those shamrock eyes when Dublin was mentioned, but Eileen had snapped back so suddenly that it might only have been caused by resentment over a visitor's meddling in household matters. Whatever the case, she obviously wasn't being coaxed to stay. She shrugged and started toward the house, consciously avoiding the front entrance. Going in that way would have brought her face to face with Drucilla's portrait. It made her edgy, feeling those eyes so like her own staring blankly down at her. Or were they blank?

Stubbornly she set her mind to other things. Let those who lived in Kilgarrom do the wondering.

Harps and wraiths and squeaks in the night were no concerns of hers!

Head down, scrunching along the path, she was almost to the kitchen door when a flash of movement inside drew her attention to the window. Two men—angry men, from the look of them—were seated at the kitchen table.

Tara's heart gave a bounce. Neal was back! But she could scarcely run and fling herself into his arms. Not in view of Rory's glowering presence. Neither was she going to back away. She pulled the door open and stepped inside just as Rory scrawled his signature across the bottom of a sheet of paper.

"Does that satisfy you, then?"

"There's no other choice. Be reasonable—"

Both men saw Tara at the same time. The confrontation came to an abrupt halt. Rory's attractive face was still tight with resentment as he brushed past her and strode outdoors. But Neal sprang quickly to his feet and clasped her in a heartfelt embrace.

"Let me look at you!" he exclaimed, dropping kisses on her upraised face. "You're the one solid thing in my world right now."

Tara wondered how she could ever have doubted his devotion. Relaxing in his arms, she told herself that nothing at all mattered except their being together. Then a slamming door somewhere in the house jerked her back to reality.

"Darling, I feel the same way about you," she murmured. "But what was that frightful scene with Rory just now? He looked like Esau, signing away his birthright for a mess of pottage."

Neal's shoulders slumped in exhaustion. His eyes shifted to the paper lying on the table. "In a way Kilgarrom did represent his heritage, I suppose. But none of us could hope to support this great albatross of a place."

Tears welled in Tara's eyes. Remembering the passionate longing that had underlain Rory's light chatter of knights and dragons the day before, she gazed pleadingly at her fiancé. "No doubt you're right. Still—couldn't you let him try? Just— transfer your interest in Kilgarrom to your cousin? He'll look after Caithlin, I'm sure. And it means so much to him!"

Neal jammed his fists into his pockets. "So you think I'm being unfair too!" Injured shock tinged every syllable.

"No," Tara said quietly. "I think it was Cormac who acted unfairly, leaving such a weighty burden on the shoulders of somebody who left Ireland twenty years ago. Rory and Caithlin—they're all the family you have left. Wouldn't it be better to leave these decisions up to them? After all, they'll have to go on living in this country long after you and I return to America."

"If only it were as simple as you make it sound." Neal dropped morosely into a chair, staring at the document Rory had signed. Frowning at it couldn't change its significance, though. As if realizing this, he turned back to Tara.

"Forgive me, *alannah,* for snapping at you. Let's take the day off. We'll drive away as if we were tourists on vacation, without a care in the world except seeing how far our travelers' checks would stretch."

"Oh, Neal, could we? You don't think anyone would mind?" Tara had been yearning for just such an opportunity. It would be their chance to talk, really talk—to try to recapture the close insight into each other's feelings they had once known.

It took her less than five minutes to change into clothes more suitable for a day in the countryside. By the time she returned to the kitchen, Neal had scrawled a short note of explanation for the family. Tara noticed that the sheet bearing Rory's signature had vanished from the table. She tried to swallow the worry that welled up once again at the thought of the cousins' animosity.

Neal gunned the motor of Cormac's elderly car as they careened down the hill. Clearly he was only too happy to be driving away from Kilgarrom and all its problems. Tara leaned back in the seat, watching his expression grow gradually more carefree. They were nearly to Longford before she remembered to ask how the auction had gone.

"Fantastic! Much better than we dared hope."

"You sold all the horses?"

Neal nodded. "Tim's going to stay on here for a bit, though, to keep things from falling to pieces. Whoever buys Kilgarrom may want to hire an experienced stableman."

So he hadn't changed his mind, Tara realized with a pang. In spite of her pleas, he was determined that the castle be sold. Opening her lips to protest, she clamped them tight against the flow of words threatening to burst forth. Neal's jaw had that set look. Another argument would only serve to spoil what was left of their day.

The farther south they drove, the rockier and more barren the land became. The lowlands had a ridged, terraced look to them, rather like a series of giant steps leading nowhere. "Peat bogs," Neal said. "The farmers spade out chunks of turf and burn it in their hearths."

"What are those lovely white flowers growing out there?"

"Bog cotton. Sort of a weed. During the war, when other materials were scarce, it was used to make parachutes. There's no commercial value in it nowadays."

Neal's expression turned glum upon hearing the motor pitch roughen. The Morris coasted to a stop just outside a tiny village. "There goes another of my best-laid plans," he grumbled. "I had planned to take you to visit Blarney Castle."

"We'll do that another time. It would be fun to hang by our heels and kiss the Blarney Stone, but truthfully, Neal, I'd rather we just sat here and talked."

"Can't do that on an empty stomach," he said. "Let's see if there's someplace here that can offer us a bit of hospitality."

No place in the town was open on Sunday except a small market. They settled for a picnic lunch of bread and cheese, carrying their makeshift meal back to the side of the road. Neal found an old blanket in the backseat, and stretched it out for them to sit on. For a half hour they were content to munch and chat about nothing in particular. At last, however, Tara brushed the crumbs from her hands and broached the subject she had been avoiding up until then.

"I'm going to Dublin tomorrow, Neal. My job has been postponed far too long already. Will you come with me? It should take only a day or two to find the information I need, and after that—" She took a deep breath. "I think it's time we went home, where we belong."

"You're asking if I'm ready to go back?"

She nodded. "We can't stay forever. Your import arrangements have all been made. And you seem to have settled the question of selling Kilgarrom." Her eyes fastened on him beseechingly. "We have the future to think about. Don't we?"

The silence between them branched out and out, like shallow ripples after a stone is dropped into a pool. For a time Tara feared that Neal did not mean to answer. When finally he did speak, there was both statement and question in his reply.

"My future belongs to no one but you, *alannah*. It's the present I can't seem to get clear of. Tell me what's been happening since I left for Athlone."

Reluctant to drag her thoughts back to Kilgarrom, yet feeling it was his right to know about the ever more perplexing events at the castle, Tara proceeded to bring him up to date. His face tightened into wary alertness when she mentioned Inspector Sheridan. Obviously the manner in which Cormac had met his death was no news to Neal, yet the policeman's continuing interest seemed a shock. It left Neal less inclined than ever to discuss his uncle's affairs.

"And then there was the seance," she added wearily.

"Seance!" Neal's head jerked up. "Don't tell me Caithlin has got you believing in her wretched ghosts too!"

"Just one. And I don't believe, not really. But honestly, Neal, when that weird harp music started echoing through the halls, I had goose bumps all over. There simply was no logical way to explain it."

With a furious motion he began shaking out the blanket. "Now you see why it's necessary for Kilgarrom to be sold. Spooks, policemen, memories of evil days—no one can live under those conditions and keep their sanity. It's a relic of superstition, not a home, and the sooner Caithlin's out of there, the better. Some historical society or school ought to be glad to take it off our hands."

Tara picked up the remains of their lunch. "And if they don't? How long will you let the 'present' of Kilgarrom keep you trapped here?"

"Not an instant longer than necessary," he said, touching her bright hair. "I'm even more anxious than you to begin our future. Can you have patience just a little while yet?"

Patience he would have, Tara agreed. But it would have been so much easier to make the promise if Neal had said even one definite word about going home. As they were passing through Ballycroom she realized that he had not even committed himself to accompanying her to Dublin the next day.

Just then his whole attention was focused on urging the Morris to labor the last mile or so, around the lake and up the hill. Tara let out her breath only when they had sputtered safely to the crest.

"Heavens, what an effort! Neal—"

Objective reached, he turned toward her. But some movement in the distance beyond her shoulder caught his eye. Violently, he jammed on the brakes. Before Tara could recover from the jolt, he had spun out of his seat and darted to the side of the road, where the timber-lined hill fell away and sloped into the south meadow.

His expression tightened into a mixture of disgust and anger.

"What is it? What's the matter?" she demanded, jumping out to join him on the verge.

Neal's glare softened not one bit. He pointed downward, and Tara swiveled, prepared for almost anything. Anything but what was actually there. Wending its way through the pasture was one of the strangest sights she had ever seen.

"But—what *is* it?" she repeated.

"Tinker folk!"

CHAPTER NINE

Tara gaped disbelievingly at the outlandish spectacle. A caravan of what appeared to be small, vividly painted Quonset huts built atop carts and drawn by horses was plodding across the field. Men swayed on raised platforms at the front of each peculiar vehicle, flapping the reins, while women trudged alongside, their wide skirts swinging in the breeze. Barefoot children and a darting, yapping pack of dogs added bulk to the parade.

Even from this distance Tara could hear the raucous uproar accompanying the wagon train's progress. Utterly bewildered, she caught Neal's arm. "It's like something out of Cecil B. De Mille! Who on earth are Tinker folk?"

"Irish gypsies." For a moment it seemed he would dash down the slope and attempt to drive

93

them off single-handedly. But there were at least a dozen burly men in the party, not to mention the swarm of dogs. Prudence restrained him.

"Tinkers are the very devil to get rid of, once they settle in," he said in disgust. "They're noisy and truculent and uneducated. Truant officers have just about given up trying to catch the children to clap them into school. And there's not a chicken or cow safe for miles around when a caravan appears. You wouldn't believe the atrocious litter surrounding their campsites."

Suddenly the procession creaked to a halt. Kettles were dragged from the interiors of wagons. Children began scurrying around, gathering scraps of wood.

"They seem to be settling down for a stay," Tara said worriedly.

Neal spun on his heel and headed back to the car. "They'll have to make other plans. We've troubles enough now, without adding gypsies to the scene."

She slid in next to him. "How do they live? Surely they can't steal everything necessary to support such a large party?"

"Oh, they do odd jobs. Sharpen knives, mend pots and pans. This and that—if it's not too much work." Neal sent the car spurting across the courtyard. The next instant his steps clattered across the cobblestones, heading for the kitchen entrance. Following more slowly, Tara could hear him shouting for Rory.

"It's back to Dublin he's gone," Brigid was saying as she entered.

Neal swore. "That leaves just Tim and myself to try and drive those squatters off!"

Dropping the ladle back into the stew pan, the old woman launched a sharp protest. "I'll not be having such language in my kitchen!"

"Not even against Tinkers?" Neal looked about to explode. "I don't suppose there's much hope of rousing the *gardai* on a Sunday night. Even if I could get that sputtering old hulk of a car to run as far as Ballycroom."

Brigid's face had gone suddenly white as flour. In spite of the animosity the woman had always shown toward her, Tara felt a surge of compassion. She placed an arm around the housekeeper's shoulders and guided her to a chair.

"Shall I come with you to fetch Tim?" she asked, swinging back to Neal. "Maybe the three of us, with Gray Boy, can bluff them off the property."

He shook his head emphatically. "No way. Stay here and keep the doors locked."

As his hurrying steps crunched down the path, Tara shot the sturdy bolt, then gave Brigid another concerned glance. "Not to worry," she said, adopting an expression she had heard a hundred times since coming to Ireland. "You'll be safe here. I'll go take care of the front door and then look in on Caithlin. Okay?"

Brigid's nod was reluctant, but she leaned back in the chair. Satisfied, Tara strode rapidly down the long corridor. She felt a trifle foolish as she locked, then brought down the heavy wooden bar across the double doors. Much good that would do if the gypsies decided to break a window and climb in!

Still, the house was as secure as she could make it. At home, she thought, there'd be the telephone with its emergency "911," and neighbors all around. Here there was no way to call for help. Kilgarrom was cut off from the rest of the world.

For once passing Drucilla's portrait without a glance, she ran up the stairs and tiptoed to the door of Caithlin's bedroom. It stood ajar. Tara pushed it open and called softly.

Neal's aunt responded immediately. Her un-braided hair fanned damply out across the pillow, and her face still bore the too-flushed appearance that had alarmed the household that morning. But she answered in a clear, lucid voice.

"Come in, my dear. Please don't think I always spend my Sundays in bed. I was just about to get up and help Brigid with the evening meal."

"You'll do no such thing. I didn't come to disturb you, only to see how you were feeling and to visit for a while."

On the pretext of adjusting the drapes, Tara glanced out the window. No disturbing view was to be had from this part of the house. Hopefully, they could avoid alarming Caithlin. With luck, Neal could shoo away the caravan before his aunt learned the gypsies had arrived in the vicinity.

Drawing a chair near the bed, she leaned forward and placed her hand on Caithlin's brow. Too warm. Feverish.

"Why don't we ask Dr. Findlay to stop by for a cup of tea?" she suggested. "Think of how much good it would do him to get out in the fresh air."

An amused smile brushed Caithlin's lips. "You suppose he needs the exercise, do you? No need; I'll be fine. Himself didn't hold much with doctors, you know. Said they were too fond of wakes to suit him."

Her eyes moved past Tara to a photograph on

the bureau. Tara studied the framed enlargement with interest. Cormac had been a rugged, good-looking man, with a glint of humor in his steady eyes and solid determination tilting his jaw.

"He wouldn't want you to lie here sick when you could be getting better."

"Cormac was a good husband. He always took care of me." Caithlin's voice sounded remote. In her mind she seemed to have slipped back to an earlier time. "Only one thing mattered more to him than me and Kilgarrom, and that was his loathing for the British. The tragedy of his youth was too strong for him to ever outgrow."

Poor Caithlin, to have lived with that vendetta for all those years, Tara thought sadly. But chances were, she had never learned of the gun smuggling until Cormac's death brought the whole affair out into the open. She wondered suddenly if Inspector Sheridan realized this. Surely he must have questioned Caithlin, and convinced himself of her innocence.

That certainty made it all the harder to understand his continuing interest in the neighborhood. Unless it was really Neal he suspected. Tara shook her head, instantly rejecting the disturbing idea. In all the time she had known him, her fiancé had never shown the slightest interest in politics, American or Irish. Why would he do so now? There was no reason. No reason at all.

Except revenge? The notion crept in, unbidden. His uncle, after all, had been killed. But that was Cormac's own fault. He had knowingly pursued his violent destiny until that final explosive encounter which had ended his life.

Caithlin made another fluttering attempt to get

up. "Oh, please don't," Tara cried in distress. "Brigid has a lovely pot of stew simmering, and Eileen should be back soon to help out too. All of us will feel much happier if we know you are resting."

"But I have rested, dear. The whole day."

Firmly, Tara tucked the bedclothes back around the older woman's shoulders. "Tomorrow, if your temperature has come down, you can wave goodbye to me from the door. I must run up to Dublin for a day or two and finish my work on the Ardill chart. How can I concentrate on doing a family tree, unless I'm sure you're on the mend?"

"Indeed, that's blackmail," Caithlin protested. Nevertheless, she settled back against the pillows with a promise to nap again until suppertime.

At least her recovery won't be hampered by fears of gypsies! Tara congratulated herself, hurrying back down the stairs. For the past few minutes she had grown steadily more apprehensive about Neal's safety, however. Turning the corner into the kitchen, she saw that Brigid was up and busy again, mixing dough for dumplings.

"Please come bolt the door behind me," she called. "I'm going to have a look around outside and see if Neal is on his way back yet. If you hear a knock, don't open up without checking that it's one of us."

"Never fear," the old woman said. "Look sharp, now. Those Tinkers have been accused of stealing away more than livestock and saddles. A pretty little thing like you— Well, you just can't trust such folk as they."

"Why, Brigid!" Tara halted on the doorsill in surprise. "That's the friendliest thing you've ever said to me. Have you gotten over being afraid I'll bring bad luck to the house?"

"Bad luck, good luck—it comes when it's ready. Just don't go giving it any cause to hurry."

When the bolt had grated into the slot behind her, Tara turned quickly down the path in the direction Neal had taken. She called once or twice, raising her voice in the futile hope that he might be close by. Then, not knowing what else to do, she climbed the slope again and picked her way along the road until she had a clear view of the gypsy encampment.

To her amazement, she saw that the caravan was on the move again. The lead wagon had swung around and was proceeding slowly toward an uncultivated plot of land beyond the far hedgerow. The other vehicles followed, escorted by the ragged convoy of children and dogs.

She jumped and almost screamed as something moist and wiggly nudged her knee. "Gray Boy, honestly! Do you always have to sneak up on me?" She reached to rumple the wolfhound's coat. "Are you the cause of those Tinkers taking to their heels like that?"

"He deserves part of the credit." Neal emerged from beneath the overhang of the verge, which had been hiding him from sight. Behind him trailed a knobby dark wisp of a man whom she recognized as Tim Foyle. "At least I can't think of any other explanation. The Tinker folk aren't short on courage, and usually it takes a whole squad of *garda* to evict them."

"Then what did happen?"

"Begged our pardon, they did, for wandering onto the property," Tim said in obvious mystification. "We'd no more than hinted at calling the law when their leader said that seeing as how they weren't welcome, they'd take themselves off."

"Not very far off. They intend to stop in that next pasture for a day or two to mend their gear." Neal shrugged helplessly. "It isn't Kilgarrom's land, so we've no right to drive them any farther. But it does seem peculiar, just the same."

"What's the difference why they left? They're gone, aren't they?" Tara pointed out practically. "Come on—let's go relieve poor old Brigid's mind. I'm sure she was expecting to be murdered in her bed, at the very least."

"They'd have had trouble with that old crone, they would," Tim said, chortling. "Pity the poor gypsy who tried to carry her off!" He veered toward the stables, calling that he would take Gray Boy with him for the night in case the Tinkers changed their minds.

Tara linked her arm through Neal's and matched her stride to his long paces. "Looks like everything is under control," she said happily. "Now we can zip off to Dublin with clear consciences."

"I suppose so. Transportation should be no problem. I've heard a bus runs through the village sometime during the morning." Neal sounded absentminded. Now and then he glanced back over his shoulder, as though still puzzling over the Tinkers' unprecedented cooperativeness.

Like Tara, Brigid was not interested in why they had decided to move on. That they had done so was all that mattered to her. It was evident that Neal had risen several notches in her estimation for having, somehow, conjured them out of the south meadow. She insisted that they sit down at once, and she ladled the choicest morsels of stew onto his plate.

Tara cajoled Brigid into having her meal while the food was hot, then cleaned her own plate quickly. "I'm going to take a dish of this broth and a boiled egg up to Caithlin," she said, busying herself at the stove. "She hasn't heard a word about the Tinkers, remember."

In minutes she was on her way up the stairs with an appetite-coaxing tray of food. She found Neal's aunt sitting up in bed looking a trifle stronger than she had that afternoon. Draping a robe around Caithlin's shoulders, Tara arranged the dishes on a bedside table.

"I hope it's still warm," she said. "Heavens, the length of those corridors! I'll keep you company, shall I? After you eat, I'll help you get settled for the night."

"What a way to spend your first visit to Ireland," Caithlin said after she had eaten a few bites. "It's glad I am that you're off to Dublin tomorrow. That's a delightful city for a young person to visit. Plenty to see and do."

"I'm looking forward to it. Have a little of the egg now." Tara kept her voice bright and cheerful. "The stew's tasty, isn't it? I hope Eileen returns before it's all gone."

"Now, there's a darlin' girl. And that busy, you wouldn't believe! But she always finds time to visit Kilgarrom. Even now, when there's no real reason for her coming."

"No real reason?" Tara echoed blankly.

A confused look crossed Caithlin's face. "You didn't know, then? Och! Silly me. I thought sure someone would have told you. Eileen is Cormac's daughter, you see."

Tara began to understand.

"Twenty-five years ago or so we were in danger of losing Kilgarrom because of the taxes. There'd been a drought; the crops failed, and money was terribly scarce. No jobs at all in this part of the country. Finally, Cormac headed up for Belfast, and turned his hand to whatever work could be found there."

After a pause, Caithlin continued, "Lonesomeness was hard on a lusty fellow like Cormac. When he came home he told me about the woman who'd befriended him. And the child." She sighed. "Mary O'Keefe passed on when Eileen was about eleven. Poor little girl—none of it was her fault. We brought her here to Kilgarrom and saw her through school. She has her own place now, and a thriving business. We've stayed on good terms."

Tara swallowed hard. Not many women would have played loving stepmother to their husband's illegitimate child. "Well, I—I think you all acted very sensibly. And even though Cormac is gone now, Eileen still has a strong reason for coming to Kilgarrom. You're as dear to her, obviously, as she is to you."

She wondered if Neal knew about this close tie binding Eileen to the family. Perhaps not. Maybe if he considered that both she and Rory were ready to assume responsibility for Caithlin, he might be less insistent about having the castle sold. She decided to suggest that to him as soon as they had a few minutes alone.

Tara spent another quarter hour in the room, drawing the draperies, tucking a freshly filled hot water bottle at Caithlin's feet, lowering the lamp. Then she loaded the half-empty dishes on her tray and balanced it carefully as she started back down the stairs.

In spite of the strong, late twilight which had brightened the bedroom, the stairwell was dim and crowded with shadows. Tara descended with caution, aware that a tumble down the uneven wooden steps could be disastrous. She had no desire to join Drucilla in haunting the place.

She wasn't more than halfway down when a ray of daylight illuminated the foot of the stairs for an instant, then just as instantly swung away and brought the shadows back. Someone had entered through the door standing opposite the empty pantry, between the kitchen and the service stairs. The next moment Eileen's voice came clearly to her ears.

"I've had a message," Eileen said in an urgent tone. "It'll be soon. Any day now. The—"

Surprise caused Tara to miss her footing. A teaspoon clattered against the egg cup; a water glass jigged drunkenly, sloshing its contents across the tray. She made a desperate grab for the banister to keep from falling. As her hand closed over the rail, she realized that the voice had ceased in midsentence.

The dishes continued to rattle as she stumbled down the last few steps. A sharp right turn brought her face to face with Neal and Eileen, standing close together just inside the pantry. Both of them wore tight, listening expressions—the look of conspirators wondering how much of their conversation had been overheard.

She caught her breath and continued on past, ignoring Neal's quick flush of guilt and the half motion he made to restrain her. Before he could say anything, Eileen was speaking again, swift, tumbling words in a tone too low to carry outside the niche where they stood.

In the kitchen, Brigid seemed unaware of any tension. She took the tray, exclaiming over the amount Caithlin had been coaxed into eating, and added that she would run up to Caithlin—just to look in, mind—before bedtime.

"Better go now," Tara said. "She was almost asleep when I left."

No more persuasion was needed to send Brigid on her way. Tara cleared the table without so much as a glance toward the pantry. Over the running of hot water into the sink she heard the back door open and close again, the thud of a bolt shooting home. Then Neal stepped into the room. He made no move to approach her. He just stood there with his clenched fists jammed into his pockets, staring at the wall over her shoulder.

"I'm sorry, Tara," he said. "Something's come up. I can't take you to Dublin tomorrow, after all."

CHAPTER TEN

As the bus jounced eastward, Tara deliberately focused her attention on the landscape. For a time the countryside was golden with odd, fan-topped haystacks, then moistly green as hills swelled up, breaking the monotony of the hedgerow-banded fields.

Already it seemed that she had been traveling half the day. First on foot, down the curving lakeside road, next aboard a swaying, horse-drawn milk cart bound for Ballycroom. The obliging farmer who had offered her a lift detoured out of his way to set her down at the bus stop near the far end of the village. After a short wait she had climbed aboard the Dublin-bound vehicle. Even then she had taken a last hopeful look around, half expecting to see Neal chugging up the narrow street to carry her off himself with a laughing explanation for last night's misunderstanding.

That hadn't happened, of course. In a way she regretted not leaving her engagement ring behind with the note she had placed on the kitchen table. But that would have posed an awkward dilemma for Caithlin. No, she'd hand it to him personally, the minute she returned to Kilgarrom to collect the rest of her luggage. End it once and for all, and be on her way back to America.

She pushed aside these unhappy thoughts as the bus swung off the rural, two-lane road and plunged onto an expressway. Within minutes they were passing through the outskirts of the capital, where the buildings were black from a hundred years or more of coal dust settling on their exteriors. Downtown, though, Dublin's aspect was cheerier. Emerald gems of parks snuggled next to aristocratic hotels. The handsome, wide streets were thronged with bustling shoppers.

Debarking with the rest of the passengers, Tara walked a short distance, trying to look at everything at once, then turned in to the first coffee shop she noticed. Brigid's stew of the night before was the last thing she had eaten. She forced herself to order something hot and to swallow it to the last morsel. In spite of the knot tightening in her throat whenever she thought about Neal, the food had an unwinding effect on her mood. By the time she came out into the street again she was ready to think of herself as a competent, working genealogist rather than as a cast-off fiancée.

She took a cab across St. Stephen's Green to Dublin Castle. Here she identified herself to a clerk and explained her errand.

"Ah, sure, and lots of folk come here searching out their forebears," the woman said. "Which sept would it be that you're after?"

Tara smiled at this seldom-used term for clan. In Scotland the clans were formal, tightly knit groups encompassing all kinfolk into one patriarchal organization. Irish family ties were more casual, further-extending links. The word "sept" described a group of people whose immediate ancestors bore a common name and inhabited the same locality.

"Since coming to America, the family has always used the name Ardill," she said. "It's quite possible, though, that two or three different spellings were used here in Ireland. I've heard mention of Ardells and Ardhills both."

"And mayhap the whole lot of them stemmed from the MacArdles of County Down," the clerk said, with a knowledgeable nod. "Try that as a last resort, though. If I were you, I'd begin with the records from County Tipperary. Any of the names you've mentioned would likely have had their origin there."

In tracing the interwoven relationships of seven generations of Ardills, Tara had, through intensive work and a great deal of persistence, positively identified Liam Eugene Ardill as the forebear who had landed at Boston Harbor on May 16, 1847. The National Archives in Washington, D.C., kept records of all ships arriving in America, and lists of the passengers aboard each vessel. It was through this source that she had confirmed the arrival from Ireland of Matthew Ardill's ascendant.

"Perhaps the sailing lists would be the place to start, if they extend that far back," Tara mused aloud after being escorted to a worktable in one of the archives rooms. "Unfortunately, the *Connaught Packer* listed several ports of call in Ireland on its manifest. The person I'm attempting to trace could have boarded the ship as far north as Cushendall or Larne. Or he may not have come aboard until Drogheda or Wicklow or even Kinsale."

The clerk looked startled. "Oh, my dear—have you nothing more to go on than that?"

"I'm afraid not," Tara said. "Liam Ardill was a young bachelor at the time of his arrival in America. Whatever written records the family had either stayed behind here, or were lost when the next generations moved west."

"What a pity! I'm afraid we can't help you." The clerk looked truly sorry. "You see, when the Public Records Office burned down in 1922 nearly all our valuable old papers and books were lost forever. If it was something more recent, or—"

"Oh, but that can't be!" Tara said. "I've written to Dublin Castle several times before, from San Francisco. This office has always been able to assist me in locating an early ancestor of a client."

"In that case, you must have been able to give us the town or at least the county where that person lived. When we know that much, we can forward the request on to someone in that particular locality. They check old church records, census lists kept in courthouses, even consult local historians. But this time—"

Tara nodded disconsolately. It was true. In the past there had always been some definite geographical clue to help in the quest. Not that it had been easy, even then. Unsettled conditions, invasions, rebellions, mass emigrations—all of these factors had contributed to the destruction or loss of vital

Irish genealogical documents. But that was a piece-meal attrition. Nothing half so devastating to the knowledge of heredity as the blaze that had reduced the compilation of centuries to ashes in a single burst of flame!

A librarian had been standing nearby, stacking tomes onto a shelf with practiced dexterity. Now she bustled over to join in their conversation.

"You've tried Fermaugh House in Belfast, haven't you?" she asked. "Their records date to before the time of Cromwell. In many cases, they have duplicates of the papers we lost in the fire."

Tara snatched eagerly at this hopeful piece of news. "Of course! I'd forgotten that was so. Thank you so much!" Then she remembered the headlines about bombings and civil war. "But can it be done? Would I be allowed to cross the border into the north counties?"

"Sure, and you an American? Nothing could be simpler. Pop on a bus and off you go. It's been fair peaceful there in Belfast of late," the librarian said encouragingly.

Emerging from Dublin Castle a few minutes later with the address of Fermaugh House tucked safely in her shoulder bag, Tara paused at a sidewalk stand to purchase a newspaper, the first she had seen since her arrival from the States. She sat down on a park bench to skim through the pages. Several items related to affairs in Northern Ireland, but none chronicled any recent violence. At the moment, the strife which for the past decade or two had consumed the six counties seemed to be at a simmer, rather than a boil.

She *could* write or telephone the archives office in Belfast, Tara supposed. But she knew from past experience how time-consuming such a process could be. Days, weeks even, might pass before they were able to furnish her with any definite information.

No, she decided abruptly, tossing the paper into a trash basket. Matthew Ardill was depending on her to gather the data as quickly as possible. It would be plain cowardice to shift the task onto others. She'd go to Belfast herself. Then, if it turned out that Fermaugh House couldn't furnish a lead to his long-ago ancestor, at least she would have done her best.

A glance at her watch showed that it was already past two o'clock. Even if she were fortunate enough to find a bus leaving immediately, there would be too little time to accomplish much today. It would be better, she decided, to plan on departing first thing in the morning. That way she could start fresh and devote the whole day to a concentrated search.

The Shelbourne Hotel was just around the corner. Captivated by its old-world charm, Tara registered and was taken up to her room by an elevator lad who looked barely old enough to be out of grammar school. After a refreshing wash, she asked the maid where the central shopping district was located.

"That would be Grafton Street, miss," the woman replied. "Just a few blocks over. You could take a taxi, I suppose, but it's a friendly day for a walk."

It was just that, Tara found. Passersby in the street were eager to give directions. One obliging person even walked along with her for a short distance to make certain she took the right turning.

Grafton Street proved to be an exciting array of specialty shops intermingled with large department stores.

Turning in at Brown and Thomas, Tara purchased several pieces of hand-cut Waterford crystal to be shipped home as gifts. At Switzers she found dainty tea towels and exquisite napery woven from thick Irish linen. Wandering happily from department to department, she chose a present for Caithlin, a woolen cardigan in a flattering shade of pink, to ward off the chill of Kilgarrom's thick walls.

Exercising her willpower, Tara bypassed the fashionably cut suits and dresses gracing the windows of Colette Modes and turned instead in the direction of O'Connell Street. She found it pleasant to amble along this, one of the widest thoroughfares in Europe, and to stand for a moment gazing up at the famous statue of Daniel O'Connell. Then she crossed the little footbridge spanning the River Liffey and smiled at the sight of swans competing with slow-moving barges for the right-of-way.

She had walked halfway back to the hotel when a familiar name lettered across a plate-glass window caught her eye. *McDermott's—Books, Records, Postal Cards,* the sign read. *Could it be?* she wondered. Entering, she knew as soon as the tall, dark-haired proprietor turned toward her that she had found the right shop.

"Hello, Rory."

"Tara!" He came forward to clasp both her hands. "Is this my lucky day, or has my cousin ruined everything by coming with you?"

It would serve no useful purpose to mention that she and Neal could no longer be considered a twosome. "I'm alone. It's a business trip, really," she said. "Unfortunately, all the documents I had planned on searching through at Dublin Castle went up in smoke sixty-five years ago. I'll be leaving for Belfast in the morning to see if I can find the information I need there."

"Belfast, is it?" Rory frowned thoughtfully. "That's a lovely drive. Let me see if I can get away from this musty shop for a day, and I'll run you up myself."

He vanished into a cubbyhole at the rear, which served as his office, and emerged ten minutes later looking exceedingly pleased. "That's settled, then. Paddy, my assistant, will tend the place while I'm gone. I'll pick you up for dinner at six-thirty, shall I? By a stroke of great good fortune I've managed to get a pair of tickets to the Abbey Theater tonight."

It ought to have been a delightful evening. The seafood supper was excellent, the performance by the Abbey Players even better. When the curtain fell on the final scene, Rory led her off to Jurys for a glimpse of the Irish Revue. All in all, Tara should have enjoyed it much more than she did. But each time she prepared to concentrate solely on Rory, Neal's grave, square-jawed visage popped up to spoil the attempt. Dolefully she wondered if, like Caithlin, she'd be haunted all her life—not by any Lady with a Harp, but by the man she had loved and lost.

Brushing her hair as she prepared for bed that night, her blond, gray-eyed mirror image recalled Drucilla again to her mind. Who had she been, that strong-willed look-alike? There was a link between them, of that she felt absolutely certain. Perhaps the clue to their relationship lay buried somewhere in the dusty archives of Fermaugh House. If she had the time—

Decisively Tara shook her head. Locating Matthew Ardill's forebears was her first concern. Nothing must be allowed to sidetrack her from that pursuit, to interfere with her professional commission. But someday—she glanced again at the face in the glass, then snapped out the light—someday she would learn the answer.

Morning traffic was just beginning to thicken as they sped northward out of Dublin the next day. Off to the right Tara caught brief glimpses of the foam-flecked Irish Sea. To the left were lonely foothills. She buttoned her coat more tightly, wishing now that she had invested in one of the warm mohair scarves she had admired yesterday.

Beside her, Rory seemed impervious to the chill. "Over there," he remarked presently, "lies the Valley of the Kings."

"Where Brian Boru held court?"

"If you could call it that. Mainly, I believe, he and his men planned various strategies to repel invaders. Between the Vikings and the Normans, they had a full-time job just doing that."

She squirmed in her seat, hoping to catch sight of Tara Hill, but fog curtained it from view. Not long afterward Rory mentioned with a challenging laugh that they were now beyond the Pale.

"You needn't think you're so smart," she responded promptly. "I know what that means. The 'Pale' was the area of eastern Ireland ruled by the British. Their jurisdiction extended over Dublin and most of the surrounding counties. Anything more distant was 'beyond the Pale.'"

One dark eyebrow raised, as if in mocking salute. "Ah, it's a pleasure to meet a girl who's so well educated. You're sure, are you, that you really prefer my cousin? We'd make a fine, intelligent pair."

"Careful, Rory. Someday a girl will take you seriously and accept one of your halfhearted proposals!"

Despite her crisp rejoinder, it was all Tara could do to conceal the aching sense of loss stirred by his banter. Wistfully she reminded herself that Neal had never actually said he preferred Eileen. It was only his actions, his secretive behavior, that had convinced her that, for him, their romance was over.

Here and there they passed large estates encircled by high stone walls. "Famine walls, those are," Rory said. "Built during the 1840s to give work to some of the starving people. There was no government aid or social welfare in those days, but a few of the landowners did what they could to help."

Tara wondered whether Liam Ardill might have helped to cement some of the heavy gray rocks into place before embarking for America. Gone now was her original reluctance to venture into the north counties. With each mile they drove she became more eager to reach Belfast. There, with luck, she might find a pointer leading to some definite indication of the man's family background.

The road swooped down to the sea again at Dundalk. Tara caught glimpses of the silky golden beaches the Irish call "strands." Within minutes they were turning inland once more. A short time later Rory slowed, then halted as the border crossing loomed ahead.

At the guard post Tara's passport was scrutinized much more thoroughly than had been the case at Shannon. Rory's papers, too, were subjected to a rigorous inspection, and the car was searched with painstaking care. Like the uniformed officers of the Republic, these policemen wore the familiar harp insignia. But here the emblem was topped by a crown, and the guards had a tough, wary look unlike the relaxed attitude so prevalent in Eire. It was a relief when the barrier was at last raised, and the car allowed to proceed.

Tara was more than a bit sobered by this grim reminder that they were entering a country torn by sporadic civil war. To be sure, it all looked peaceful enough. But Rory, too, seemed definitely on edge. His jaw had a tightness about it that did not loosen until the road climbed and began to curl through the Mountains of Mourne.

Belfast was brick from one end to the other, the streets an endless repetition of themselves. Long rows of houses stretched out on both sides of the main thoroughfare, as featureless as pieces on a Monopoly board, each one with its peaked roof and identical tier of steps and blank brick facade.

"Good heavens!" she exclaimed. "How do the people find their way home at night?"

"It takes a good head for numbers," Rory said with a grin. "Forget your house address, and you're just another voice crying in the wilderness."

The city center had a solid, prosperous appearance, but it lacked the good-natured bustle of Dublin. Pedestrians strode briskly from point to point.

Few paused outside store windows; no smiles were exchanged between passersby. To Tara, the ring of red and yellow flowers encircling the statue of Queen Victoria in the main square was like a brave anthem or a flag held high. The blossoms were the only touch of brightness or cheer she noticed anywhere in Belfast.

Once inside Fermaugh House, however, all thoughts of the present dropped away as she lost herself in the files of an earlier century. A helpful archivist quickly located a folder of records kept of the coffin ships that had sailed from Irish ports in the 1840s. Tara turned to the tab marked "1847" and paged through, scarcely realizing that she was holding her breath until the name *Connaught Packer* leaped out at her.

The skipper had apparently been eager to fill every square foot of space with living cargo: Hundreds of persons were listed as having boarded at the three most northerly ports. But no familiar name appeared among this group. Biting her lip, she turned the page, peering at the faded, cramped writing which identified those who had taken passage at Wicklow.

There it was. Not one Ardill, but two: Liam and Sean.

For a moment she could only stare dumbfounded at the page. She herself had examined the emigration list at the National Archives in Washington, D.C. Liam was the only Ardill to arrive in Boston Harbor aboard the *Connaught Packer*. Never would she have overlooked something so obvious!

Almost at once, then, the logical explanation occurred to her. The vessels that plied the Atlantic in those days had really earned the name "coffin

ships." Many persons who embarked upon a
voyage did not live to celebrate the end of it. So it
was quite possible that two Ardills had started out
together.

Tara leaned back in the chair, trying to contain
her excitement. Unless the repetition of the name
were a mistake or mere coincidence, this discovery
could be a real bonanza. If Liam and Sean had been
related, she now had two leads, two distinctive
Christian names, to follow. The Ardill family she
sought would be twice as traceable!

Unfortunately, the ship's manifest furnished no
addresses for its passengers. But in her past research Tara had found that, unlike Americans, Irish
families tended to remain in the same area for generations. All she had to do was find the *right* area.
And for this the librarian at Dublin Castle had already given her a lead that might prove invaluable.

"This was exactly what I needed to begin my
search." Smiling, she returned the passenger lists
to the archivist. "Now, do you know if a census of
County Tipperary was taken during the early
1840s?"

Again she was in luck. Although it was not a particularly common name, Tara located nearly a
dozen branches of the sept Ardill, all clustered in
one general vicinity. From the census report she
proceeded to township rolls and finally to old
church records.

It was this last source that brought a sparkle to
her tired eyes. Both Liam Eugene Ardill and his
younger brother Sean had been baptized in the par-
ish church of Cashel. The parents of the boys were
also listed. Some terrible tragedy must have over-
taken the family in 1846: Mother, father, and two

sisters were listed as having been buried from the church late in that year. In an earlier entry she found a notation of the parents' marriage. From this point it was a relatively simple task to trace the lineage back to the latter part of the 1600s.

Afternoon shadows had begun to fill the room by the time she at last straightened up. Jubilation over the day's work made her forget all about her aching back. Her notebook was filled with precise jottings —names, dates, relationships—tracing Matthew Ardill's ancestry back for three hundred years.

Poor Sean! she thought. *He was only sixteen when he and Liam boarded the ship. I wonder if he fell ill during the voyage, or whether he was washed overboard in a storm?*

She would never know, of course. Tantalizing questions such as these were an inevitable drawback to her profession. But futile or not, she couldn't hold back a stab of sadness for the lad who had died somewhere between Ireland and America.

A glance at the wall clock brought her sharply back to the present. When leaving her off at Fermaugh House that morning, Rory had promised to return at four-thirty. It was nearly that time now. With profuse thanks to the archivist for her help, Tara quickly made her way back to the sidewalk.

They should have reckoned with the afternoon rush hour, she thought in dismay, eyeing the jammed street. Cars swept past in a bewildering stream. How would Rory ever be able to stop long enough to pick her up?

Standing near the curb, Tara tried to watch both directions at once. A variety of blue autos sped by; none paused. The choking exhaust fumes were making her head spin. Debating whether it would be wiser to climb partway back up the steps of Fermaugh House where she could more easily see and be seen, Tara backed away. Indecisively, then, she turned once more to stare out at the street.

The double row of cars was for the moment at a standstill, poised in anticipation of the just-now-changing traffic light. There was, she thought in annoyance, every make of auto imaginable out there—dignified gray Bentleys, a green Morris or two, Ford Consuls in a rainbow of colors, even a bright red MG. Everything but a blue Rover.

The signal changed; wheels turned. The color was so vivid, so eye-catching, that Tara gave the MG a second glance as it rolled toward her, gaining velocity. The notion flashed into her mind that it was remarkably like Eileen's car. Same year, same model, same tiny tear in the convertible top. . . . For a split second it was directly opposite, not ten feet away. Suddenly, then, the resemblance didn't seem remarkable at all.

Because it *was* Eileen's car. And there on the passenger seat beside her sat Neal!

CHAPTER ELEVEN

The raucous blare of a horn jerked Tara out of her daze. Blinking, she saw Rory's car hovering at the curb. To the intense displeasure of the drivers stalled behind him, he was leaning across the seat, holding the door half open for her. She darted forward and slid onto the leather upholstery just in time for him to change gears and shoot through the light as it turned red.

He glanced in the rearview mirror, eyeing the disgruntled motorists left behind at the signal. "For a minute there I was convinced you'd turned to stone like the other statues out there."

"I'm sorry." Tara bent low, placing her purse on the floor, unbuttoning her coat—anything to keep her face hidden until she managed to get her expression under control. "I'd been staring at that

121

street until all the cars seemed to merge into one bad-smelling blur."

"Not to worry. We're safe away now, with the others stuck."

His boyish glee at having escaped the horn-honkers brought a wisp of a smile to Tara's stiff mouth. That was better. Now, if only she could keep from thinking about Neal and Eileen! She forced her voice into a carefree-sounding lilt. "Did you have a good day?"

"Passable, considering it was spent in Belfast. At least the pubs here serve Guinness instead of English ale." He quirked a sideways glance at her. "And you? Another gold star for the genealogist?"

"Yes, I was unbelievably lucky. All the information was there—everything I needed."

"Is that a fact? Standing there by the steps, with your face white as pudding, I felt sure you'd had some terrible disappointment."

Blast him and his sharp eyes! "I expect it was a mixture of gasoline fumes and hunger," she seized on a half-truth. "In the excitement of tracing the Ardills I forgot all about lunch."

"Sure, and the next thing you know we'll be building a famine wall for your benefit." Rory mentioned an inn situated a short distance outside the city, and suggested that they stop there for dinner.

Deciding she'd feign an appetite if necessary, Tara tensed when they turned into the parking lot, readying a quick excuse in case a jaunty red MG should have arrived before them. But none of the cars looked remotely familiar.

No effort at make-believe was needed after all when the savory steak-and-kidney pie was set before them. Stimulated by the delicious aroma, Tara found that she was more than ready to eat. Little by little she relaxed, consciously blotting out the memory of Neal and his betrayal.

"Tell me about your shop," she said, straining to keep Rory's attention off family matters. "Have you owned it long? From the number of bookstores I noticed in Dublin, there must be a tremendous amount of competition for customers."

"There is that," Rory said soberly. "I've had the place six years or so now, and it's a fair location. A good many tourists pop in to buy postal cards and maps."

It would take a great many of those trifles to pay the rent, Tara realized. It occurred to her that he was probably not very well off financially. Though grateful for the convenience, she was sorry now that she had allowed him to make the trip with her. Gasoline was terribly expensive here, and a meal at this lovely inn certainly couldn't be cheap. If her companion had been an American man in a similar position, she would have quietly found a way to pay her share of the check. But Irish males weren't accustomed to such a liberated outlook. Such an attempt would be bound to wound his pride.

Tactfully refusing dessert, Tara gazed in appreciation around the room while Rory signaled for the check. The hot food had done her morale a world of good. When they had first entered she had been too tense and heartsore to be aware of anything or anyone. Now she noticed that despite the early hour the majority of the other tables were occupied. Couples formed most of the clientele, although there was a sprinkling of larger parties and one or two persons dining alone. Her glance flickered over a solitary man seated near the hearth.

The next instant her attention had become not casual but intent.

Rory pointedly cleared his throat. "This place isn't old enough to be haunted. Whoever it is you're staring at so raptly can't be a ghost."

"What? Oh, no—no, he isn't." Feeling oddly disturbed, Tara forced her gaze away from the table for one. "That's Inspector Sheridan. I told you about him, remember? The policeman who came to Kilgarrom last week and asked me all sorts of questions."

"Is it, indeed?" Rory's eyes flashed briefly across the room. "Has he been here long?"

"I've only just noticed him. Why—"

About to wonder aloud why the officer should be so far from his own bailiwick, Tara bit back the words in midquestion. Chances were, she knew the answer already.

Rory didn't seem to notice the interruption. "Why is he here, do you mean? Well, the food's good. I suppose even policemen get a day off every now and then."

That could be the explanation, she agreed, allowing Rory to take her arm and guide her toward the exit. She really hoped it was the right answer. It was so much cheerier a guess than the one that had popped into her own mind.

But once they were on the road again she wondered whether accepting Rory's interpretation wasn't just a case of burying her head in the sand. Policemen with days off usually went home to Mrs. Policeman and her apple pie, didn't they? Unless there was a reason for their being someplace else. For instance, following an American who just happened to be going to Belfast? The bright color of the little red MG made it exceptionally easy to track. Perhaps it was parked near the inn. Two or three other restaurants were situated along that section of road. That was an awfully good reason, she admitted to herself—if the American in question was suspected of being a member of the outlawed IRA.

Her heart gave an aching wrench. Those suspicions simply couldn't be correct! Neal wasn't a man to become involved in intrigue. He'd never—

Tara swallowed hard. That wasn't true—not really. She was making excuses, which was just as bad as lying out loud. Ever since she'd arrived in Ireland, Neal *had* been involved in something. Some secret activity that he wouldn't or couldn't divulge. When she came right down to it, intrigue was a perfect description of his behavior.

Yet no matter how inexplicable his actions, Neal wouldn't conspire to harm innocent people. Cormac had. He'd smuggled guns and bullets and probably bombs, for that matter. No one could convince her that this was a case of like uncle, like nephew. Cormac's beliefs had been warped by years of festering hatred.

Maybe, she thought, Eileen had inherited a tinge of the same sickness. She'd lived in Belfast as a child. And Eileen was Cormac's daughter. It was all too possible that Neal had succumbed to her charm, then been deluded into thinking that he was taking part in a harmless adventure. Now it seemed probable that the police were watching his every move. Regardless of what had happened, she had to warn him—and quickly, before he became entangled in a situation so deadly he could never break free!

Tara felt chilled through and through. Shivering, she turned to Rory. "How long will it take us to reach Kilgarrom?"

"Three hours. Less, if the road stays clear." His voice sounded preoccupied as though he, too, had been deep in his own thoughts. He bore down on the accelerator and shot a watchful glance at the rearview mirror.

No sirens or flashing red lights hindered their progress. Traffic, now that they were well away from the city, seemed sparse. The Rover's powerful engine throbbed steadily, hurtling them down valleys and up hills at a rapid pace. Nevertheless, to Tara the journey seemed endless. The late summer twilight lingered on and on, giving the impression that time stood still.

At last the outlines of Lough Duneen crept into view. Was it only a week ago, she wondered incredulously, that she had approached Kilgarrom for the first time? On that evening she had scarcely been able to contain her excitement at the thought of being reunited with Neal. All that had counted then was being in his arms again. Now, she told herself, her anxiety was not to feel his embrace, but rather to issue an urgent warning—and say good-bye.

"Are you staying overnight?" she asked, making a desperate attempt to hold back her tears.

With a shake of his head, Rory braked to a halt in the cobbled courtyard. "No, it's straight back to Dublin for me. Business as usual tomorrow, worse luck."

On impulse, she stretched out her hand. "Thank you for everything, Rory. You're—you're absolutely the nicest cousin I've ever known."

There was no hint in his grave expression of the sardonic, teasing man she had begun to know and like. His strong fingers closed over hers. They clung for the space of a half-dozen heartbeats. "Good-bye, Tara," he said finally.

She stood staring after the car until its taillights disappeared around the curve. The pressure of his hand was still warm on hers. Instinctively she knew that behind those ordinary-sounding words lay regret for an emotion that had sprung into being too late.

When even the engine's hum had receded into the distance, she sighed and turned toward Kilgarrom. How badly everything was turning out! Perhaps, as well as haunting the castle, Drucilla had flung a curse on the place and all who came near it. Tara almost smiled as this notion entered her mind. Had a single week in Ireland changed her as much as that? To the point where she was ready to accept the possibility of spirits and evil spells? Not really, she supposed. Still, there was no denying that the ancient building seemed to have a star-crossed effect on romance.

She tried to plan the upcoming scene with Neal. What could she say? "Flee—all is discovered?" No, that was for telegrams. It didn't cover the contingency of ex-fiancées taking the first plane home, either.

It suddenly struck Tara that there was no need to rehearse the speech just yet. For neither on the hillside verge nor anywhere in the wide, silent courtyard was there any sign of a red MG. Peering around, she frowned in perplexity. If, when she caught that glimpse of them outside Fermaugh House, Neal and Eileen had been on their way back to Kilgarrom, they should have arrived by now. They might, of course, have stopped off somewhere. Remembering Inspector Sheridan, her throat tightened. They might even be in jail!

She rejected the notion immediately. People weren't arrested without good reason. And even though her suspicions that Eileen intended to carry on Cormac's smuggling activities were growing stronger every hour, the girl would scarcely have had the audacity to convey the contraband directly to Belfast. Not with the inch-by-inch inspection being given every vehicle to cross the border. Had the excursion to the north counties been a trial run, a test to see how rigorous the guards' precautions were?

She was too tired, too hurt to go on speculating any longer. Dejectedly, she tramped around to the side entrance. The door was locked, but a light burned in the kitchen. Presently, Brigid came shuffling around to admit her.

Underneath the shawl the old woman's white hair looked wispier than ever. Her eyes were dull from worry and lack of sleep. "Oh, miss, it's you! Come in, come in. It's glad I am that you're back."

Tara shot the bolt behind her. "What's the trouble? Is Caithlin all right?"

"Her cough is worse, poor thing, and she's breathing heavier. Yesterday Eileen brought Dr. Findlay up, even though herself said not to. He left some medicine. After taking a dose, she seemed to rally round. But now I can't persuade her to swallow it again."

Gray Boy had draped himself at the head of the stairs. Hurrying upward, Tara heard the excited thud of his tail on the landing. He nudged her hand in welcome, then trotted ahead of her into the sickroom.

Caithlin's feverish eyes stared back at her from the bed. With Brigid hovering anxiously in the doorway and Gray Boy quivering in expectation at her side, Tara perched beside the sick woman and smoothed a cool hand over her brow. The skin burned under her fingertips.

"Is it really you, Tara?" Caithlin asked hoarsely. "I thought you were off to Dublin."

Reassuringly she bent closer. "It's me. I saw all the sights and brought you a present. Now I've come back to take care of you."

They were all three watching her, waiting for her to do something sensible. Tara drew her hand away with all the calm she could pretend, and reached for the box of capsules on the bedside table.

"I don't want those things," Caithlin protested, but a racking cough spoiled the vigorous effort.

Tara scanned the prescription directions. One every four hours, along with three spoonfuls of the liquid. Trying to keep from trembling, she tipped an inch or two of water into the glass, and fished a capsule from the box.

"How can I tell you about Dublin if you keep on coughing? Here, I'll help you sit up. That's better. Now, we'll propose a toast and you drink it down." She was chattering nervously, wondering what on earth she could do if Caithlin continued to refuse the medication. "In America we might say 'down the hatch.' Here it's what—*Slainte?*"

Miraculously, the capsule was accepted. Now there was just the liquid to be coaxed into her. "Oh, I know a better one. My father always said, 'Here's to the harp of old Ireland.' Who could pass up a toast like that?"

Three times with only a little more urging the liquid disappeared from the spoon. "That's nothing to toast with. Even Scotch tastes better." Caithlin grimaced, but her feverish eyes twinkled.

Now that the ordeal was over Tara, too, could smile at her foolishness. She helped Caithlin slide back beneath the covers. Then, on the pretext of refilling the hot-water bottle, she slipped out into the hall for a look at her watch. Amazingly, it was not quite nine o'clock.

"She will need to take the medicine again in four hours," she whispered to Brigid. "I'll sit up with her until then. Get some rest, now, before you get sick yourself."

Brigid drew her shawl tighter. "Humph. I know better than to go rummaging around nasty damp attics!" Nevertheless, she shuffled off in the direction of her room. At the end of the hall she peered back with as near a chuckle as Tara had ever heard her use. "That was a fine, clever trick. 'Down the hatch,' was it?"

"That was all I could think of. Good night."

Caithlin's eyes were closed when Tara returned to the sickroom, but she was still half awake. "It's a fair city, Dublin," she mused reminiscently.

"Yes, very." The hot-water bottle was tucked snugly in place. "If you'll go to sleep, I'll tell you all about it later."

Tara dimmed the lamp, then sank down in a nearby chair and loosened her coat. Gray Boy curled up, a warm lump the size of a coal stove near her feet. It would have been a peaceful scene except for Caithlin's harsh, labored breathing, but gradually the medication took effect and the gasping breaths became easier. Absently ruffling the wolfhound's fur, Tara speculated on what Brigid had meant about rummaging around in attics. If Caithlin had done such a silly thing in her weakened condition, it was no wonder she had suffered a relapse.

The chair was deep and roomy, much too comfortable. It had been a long day. Tara found herself drifting into a doze despite her resolution to stay alert. She jerked upright and, with a wide stare, conducted a mental exercise, naming as many of the Ardill ancestors as she could remember from her research.

But even this was soporific. Her eyelids drooped, closed. A minute later she was deep in slumber.

She couldn't imagine, at first, what it was that had awakened her. A noise of some kind, she decided, darting a quick, frightened look toward the bed. But Caithlin's breaths came soft and regular; she'd made no sound. It was then that Tara glimpsed the dark silhouette at the window. As stiffly as a sentry on guard duty Gray Boy was poised there, peering down at the moonlit courtyard. A low, menacing growl, companion to the one which had stirred her from sleep, rumbled in his throat as she tiptoed across the room.

It was a clear night, with a full quota of stars and a brilliant moon. Tara plucked the curtain aside, uneasily eyeing the empty cobblestones, the sweeping driveway, the angular house front with its bulge of turret at either end. Were the Tinkers still encamped nearby? Had Brigid remembered to lock and bar the front door?

A shadow where no shadow belonged drifted dim and silent away from the mossy verge. The most that Tara could distinguish was that it was two-legged—and muscular.

"Come on, boy," she whispered, retreating toward the door.

Gray Boy followed unhesitatingly. Huge as he was, his lithe movements made less sound than her own quiet steps as together they descended the main staircase. To her relief the wooden bar was in place, barricading the heavy double doors. But there were too many windows to check quickly, nor was there any way to summon help if the prowler gained entry. Tara had only one weapon. She used it.

Lifting the bar, she unlocked the door and eased it open. "Go get him!" she ordered the wolfhound. "Give him a scare he won't forget!"

The dog was gone, streaking swiftly through the gap before the last words had left her lips. Another savage growl drifted back to her. Then . . . nothing.

Tara stepped out, pulling her coat more snugly closed against the midnight chill. Both man and dog had disappeared. She waited, expecting at any instant to hear a furious bark, thudding footsteps, a shout. So completely was her attention riveted on the wolfhound and the quarry he pursued that the more mundane sound of an engine whining up the hill did not even penetrate her consciousness until it was too late to dart back inside.

Tires squealed, gears clanged. Tara was floodlighted against the door by powerful twin yellow beams!

CHAPTER TWELVE

Blinded by the dazzling glare, Tara flung up an arm to shield her eyes. "Gray Boy, come back!" she cried frantically. The echoing cry acted as a release from the paralysis of fear keeping her rooted to the doorstep. She pivoted around, but before she could gain the safety of the house, a stronger force prevented her from moving. Neal had her shoulders surrounded by his arms.

"*Alannah!* Stop struggling!" he insisted, drawing her to one side of the lighted circle. "That's better," he added, when they had gained the shadows and her eyes focused on him with recognition. "Now— what's the trouble? And why are you out here at this time of night?"

"There was a man. We saw him from upstairs."

The terror drained away, leaving her numb and trembling. "Gray Boy went after him."

As if reporting back on cue, the wolfhound loped toward him. Neal stood still, waiting until the fierce-looking creature identified his scent as someone belonging to the household. Then he bent to dislodge a scrap of rough material that had been clenched between the dog's teeth.

Neal's laugh sounded forced as he held the triangular shred in the light for Tara to see. "Your prowler has a taste for shabby denims. He and what's left of his trousers are probably in the next township by now."

While he strode back across the courtyard to douse the car lights, Tara gave Gray Boy an approving hug. "Good fellow!" she praised, running her hands down his heaving sides. His coat was matted with burrs and thistles, as though he had indeed just finished a cross-country race.

Moments later they were inside, Neal pausing to secure the door behind them. The disruption seemed to leave them with nothing to say. Tara rewarded Gray Boy with a handful of biscuits. Neal meanwhile prowled restlessly from window to door, seemingly unable to settle anywhere.

The silence stretched on and on, becoming every second more awkward, more alive with unspoken thoughts. "Where's Eileen?" Tara asked at last, thinking of the red MG parked in the courtyard.

Neal jammed his hands in his pockets. "Home in bed, I should think."

"Getting a well-earned rest after that long trip to Belfast?" She regretted the words the instant they popped out. The question sounded so spiteful, so unlike her. But there was no calling it back.

He gave her a startled glance. "What do you know about Belfast?"

"That you were there—with Eileen. I saw you." She dropped her eyes to Gray Boy so Neal, standing so strangely still, would not notice the brightness in them. "I wasn't the only one. Inspector Sheridan was above the border too."

When he continued to say nothing she detailed the skein of circumstances that had led her from Dublin Castle to Fermaugh House. "I was standing near the curb waiting for Rory when the two of you drove by," she concluded the tale. "Neal, I—I'm afraid for you. The police are watching—"

His face looked whiter, angrier than she had ever seen it. "Is that how you've figured it out? That we're a lawbreaking pair, Eileen and I?"

"If that's not the truth, tell me what is! Tell me what's going on around here!"

For a moment Tara believed he meant to take her into his arms, kiss away her fears, and explain how completely mistaken her suspicions had been. The temptation to do so was achingly clear in every plane of his face. He even took a step forward. Then his hands dropped to his sides and he turned back to the window.

"We went to see an architect," he murmured. "The firm that shored up Kilgarrom after the landslide has its main office in Belfast now. The ground's been dropping away a little more each year. Safety factors had to be checked before we could offer the place for sale."

"I see." Tara gave Gray Boy a last pat and stood up. "It's time for Caithlin's medicine. She's been terribly sick. As soon as she's out of danger I'm leaving, Neal. Going home to San Francisco."

"I wish. . . ." He sighed and left the thought suspended. "Let me know when you're ready to go. I'll see that you get to the airport safely."

It took every grain of willpower Tara could muster to hold her head high as she walked past Neal and up the worn rear stairs. Had he really expected her to believe that thin story about an architect? Apparently, it wasn't only his love for her that had died. Trust had also disappeared. He hadn't told her the truth—but he had made it abundantly clear that he wanted her to leave Kilgarrom. Well, she could tell when she wasn't wanted. She'd see to it that he got his wish.

Marching into the bathroom, she splashed her face with water until her brimming eyes had ceased to smart. Then she tiptoed into the sickroom.

Four hours' sound sleep along with the penicillin had worked wonders for Caithlin's condition. She opened her eyes when Tara entered and took the next dose unprotestingly. Then she lay back in the bed. But sleep did not immediately return.

Sitting down next to her, Tara noticed that the stubborn cough had subsided. If she went to bed now, she would only toss and turn and weep over Neal. Caithlin's company was infinitely preferable to her own anguished thoughts.

"Were you able to finish the family tree?" the older woman asked.

"Not as far back as Adam and Eve. But I did trace the Ardills' lineage for nearly three hundred years."

"Sure, and I wouldn't have had the patience. But it's a wonderful thing, knowing who your people were." Her eyes fastened on Tara's face. "I haven't been able to get over how much you resemble the Lady with the Harp."

"Yes, it's amazing, isn't it? If I'd had more time to spend with those old records, I might have been able to find a link between Drucilla and some branch of my mother's family."

"There's bound to be a blood tie somewhere. I located some papers in a cedarwood chest in the attic. Maybe they will help a little. Drucilla's sons wrote down her songs and poems, you know. They also preserved bits of her diary."

Tara's heart pounded with excitement. "She actually kept a diary?"

"She did. I read only a page or two. The writing's badly faded, I'm afraid. But your young eyes can make it out. All the papers are over there on the bureau. I want you to have them."

Tara was already on her way across the room. Almost reverently, she picked up the box of yellowed, brittle sheets. The chest must have been airtight, she thought in wonder, to have preserved its contents so well.

If anything ever were to keep her thoughts from dwelling on Neal, this was it! "Oh, thank you," she breathed. "This is a marvelous find! But please don't go near the attic again. Nothing is worth risking a second bout with pneumonia."

"There is no need to go back now," Caithlin said, with a quiver of sadness in her voice. "Kilgarrom is to be sold. I suppose that's the sensible course. Cormac was the last of the Fitzgarths. Once I've left there will be no one to care whether Drucilla walks through these halls or not."

"Then perhaps she'll stop walking. It's time she went to join Kevin." In the middle of the night, caught up in Caithlin's mood, it was not hard to give credence to her superstitious beliefs. Tara was unable to repress a shudder as she recalled the night of the seance. It hadn't been hard then, either. The way the candle had poofed out, the eerie chords echoing through the castle. . . .

Suddenly she remembered what it was she had been intending to ask. "Caithlin, did you ever actually *see* Drucilla? Or was it just the harp music that convinced you she was still here in spirit?"

"Not only the harp. The lamps would be lit one moment and not the next. And footsteps moved beyond the wall where no human feet could tread."

"You never really *saw* anything, though?" Tara wasn't quite sure why this point should seem so important.

"She was close. So close. She never quite appeared, no. But I knew from the portrait and the old stories Cormac would tell that it was the Lady with the Harp who interrupted our peace. Seeking peace herself, she was."

Tara had a shivery impulse to turn the lamp up as high as it would go, to banish every shadow in the room. Instead, she plumped up Caithlin's pillows. "Fine pair we are, telling ghost stories at this hour! Now—to practical matters. Will you promise to take your medicine for Brigid, or shall I set my clock for five?"

"Please don't do that. I'll swallow the horrid stuff. Get some rest. You look about done in, yourself."

When she stretched out in her own room Tara did not expect to sleep. Concern for Neal and distress at his rejection vied with eager speculation as to what Drucilla's diary would reveal. Perhaps because her thoughts were so fragmented, she drifted off almost at once.

Warm sunlight awakened her. She lay still for a time, listening to the muted household noises, before remembering this was to be her last day at Kilgarrom. This afternoon she would present her gift, thank Caithlin for her hospitality, and walk down to the village. From Ballycroom she would phone the airport, arrange for a flight home tomorrow. And also find out about bus transportation to Shannon. That long drive alone in a car with Neal would be too difficult to endure.

The engagement ring still sparkled on her left hand. She started to remove it, then pushed it back in place. The other women would be sure to notice its absence, ask questions she could not bear to answer. Better to return it privately to Neal at the moment of departure.

The box of papers Caithlin had given her lay untouched on the nightstand. She glanced longingly at it as she dressed and tidied the room, but resisted the temptation to peruse its contents just yet. Once she began, she wanted time to read the pages through undistracted. Making out the faded lines of Drucilla's diary would be an ideal way to pass the long evening hours.

To her relief, both Neal and the red MG had disappeared by the time she came downstairs. There was only Molly in the kitchen to give her a cheery greeting.

"Good morning," Tara replied. "Have you heard how Caithlin is today? I sat up late with her. She seemed to be out of danger by the time I went to bed."

"Not to worry," Molly said reassuringly. "Brigid

took an egg and a bit of porridge up to herself an hour ago. She's that improved, thank the Lord."

So, Tara reflected, there was no excuse left to delay her departure. She inquired about public telephones, and was told one could be found at the Ballycroom post office. She made the decision to walk down and make her call immediately.

Beyond the hedgerow fencing off Kilgarrom's south meadow from the neighboring property she could see the brightly colored gypsy caravan. The Tinkers were taking their time about moving on. But she had no intention of copying their behavior. She found the post office with no difficulty. Half an hour later she was on her way back up the hill with a confirmed reservation on the next afternoon's Aer Lingus flight to New York, and a ticket on the bus to Shannon departing from Ballycroom at nine in the morning.

At lunchtime she carried a tray to Caithlin's room. "My, you do look better!" She noted the freshly braided hair and the eyes which had lost their feverish glint. "See what happens when you take your medicine?"

While the older woman ate, Tara described the day she had spent in Dublin. She praised the young dancers who had performed at Jurys, and sketched the plot of the offbeat play by Brendan Behan that she and Rory had seen at the Abbey Theater.

"I taught school in Dublin when I was a young woman," Caithlin said. "I've decided to return there after Kilgarrom is sold. It shouldn't be hard to find a small flat, just big enough for Brigid and myself. What would you think of my helping out at a nursery school?"

"What a grand idea! It will be nice to picture you

in a fun place like that when I'm back home in California." Tara dropped her eyes, then forced herself to continue in an ordinary tone. "I've been meaning to tell you. My vacation is almost over. Neal intends to stay on and keep you company for a while longer, but I really do have to get back to my job. I'll be leaving tomorrow."

Caithlin looked genuinely distressed. "So soon? My dear, you've only just arrived."

"It seems that way to me too, but that's because I've enjoyed your hospitality so much." Excusing herself for a moment, Tara hurried down the hall to her own room. The break gave her a chance to regain her composure. She returned carrying the gift-wrapped sweater she had purchased in Dublin.

"I hope this fits. Here, slip it over your shoulders. Pink is a marvelous color for you," she chattered brightly, holding up a hand mirror so Caithlin could see the effect.

Somehow, Tara allowed herself to be thanked and managed to get out of the room before bursting into tears. Deliberately using the front staircase to avoid encountering Molly or Brigid, she slipped outside and whistled for Gray Boy. He was exactly the companion she needed to keep her thoughts off serious subjects. After a long romp through the fields with him, she was only too glad to sink down for a rest in the tall grass, convinced that she could now get through the rest of the day without breaking down.

Nevertheless, she delayed her return to the castle as long as possible. Her perch on the hillside afforded an almost intimate view of the Tinkers' camp. Women and children moved busily about the wheeled huts. The men seemed to be lounging about doing nothing in particular. She wondered if they had already canvassed the neighborhood for knives to sharpen and kettles to mend. There was no sign of such activity going on now.

It wasn't until she glimpsed Molly riding her bicycle down the hill that she felt impelled to stir. With the wolfhound trotting along beside her, she circled around in back of Kilgarrom, taking a shortcut through the disheveled little cemetery. The half-toppled tombstones reminded her of Drucilla's diary waiting upstairs. Eyes glowing in anticipation, she quickened her steps.

But there proved to be no time to do any reading before the evening meal. Gray Boy's usually sleek coat was once again a tangle of burrs. She found a stiff brush in the kitchen and sat down on the back steps to curry him. It occurred to her that just last night she had removed an identical prickly assortment of foliage from his fur. The coincidence made her wonder whether their midnight prowler might not have been chased back to the Tinker camp, along the same fields through which she and the dog had wandered today.

Neal had still not returned by the time dinner was ready. Sitting down with only Brigid for company, Tara finished up quickly. Afterward, she opened the door and let Gray Boy outside. "Keep your eyes open," she cautioned him.

At last able to return to her room, she pulled a chair over to one of the wide windows overlooking the courtyard and seated herself there with the precious box of papers Caithlin had resurrected from the attic. From past research in libraries and museums she was accustomed to the odd spelling and old-fashioned script of seventeenth- and eighteenth-century documents. Even so, she found the time-bleached writing on these pages more difficult to decipher than expected. Wishing she had a magnifying glass to enlarge some of the almost illegible passages, she leafed through to what seemed to be the earliest entry.

To her acute disappointment, the fragment of diary began about a year after Drucilla's marriage. By then she had already been alienated from her kinfolk. There seemed little chance that she would mention her father or other relatives by name. Tara sighed but read on, fascinated by the English girl's practical outlook and her careful supervision of Kilgarrom's reconstruction financed by the ransom her family had paid for her release. By the medium of brittle paper and fading ink, Drucilla's thoughts leaped across the centuries.

Torn away from the pages only by the need to light the lamp, Tara remembered her manners and hurried down the hall to bid Caithlin good night.

"Forgive me for not having spent more time with you," she said apologetically. "I started reading Drucilla's diary and forgot about everything else. Have you taken your capsule?" When Caithlin shook her head, Tara groaned in mock distress and filled the water tumbler. "Down the hatch. Here's mud in your eye."

Caithlin laughed so hard she began to cough. "'Mud in your eye?' What happened to *Slainte?*"

"That goes with this liquid toddy, of course. Open up."

"I'll remember you and your foolish toasts whenever I have to take medicine again," Caithlin declared. "Are you really sure you must leave?"

"Positive," Tara answered steadily. She had already resolved there would be no more tears to-night. "But I'll always have fond memories of you and—and the others, here at Kilgarrom."

As she moved around the room making Caithlin comfortable for the night, she thought once she detected the faint throb of a car motor. The courtyard was still empty, however. If an auto had passed, it must have been driven by someone taking the long route around Lough Duneen. Annoyed by her depressed yearnings, she told herself firmly that her only interest in Neal lay in returning his ring.

"See you in the morning," she promised Caithlin.

Refusing to allow herself to go on thinking of Neal out enjoying himself with Eileen, she stoically returned to her room and Drucilla's manuscript. She picked up where she had left off and plunged back into the mid-1700s.

The diary changed in tone as soon as Drucilla learned that she was to bear a child. Her every thought seemed to be focused on Kilgarrom's future heir. Dates between the entries widened. A month, then two, elapsed from one jotted paragraph to the next. At the top of a fresh page Tara found the information that the couple had been blessed by the birth of twin sons:

> With what exquisite pleasure I remember my childhood with my own twin brother. We must take pains to ensure that our boys have every advantage that was bestowed on Dunstan and me, and more, besides.

Tara sprang out of her chair with a muted whoop of joy. Dunstan was a name repeated again and again in the Wentworth family Bible. Moreover,

Wentworth twins appeared with regularity, cropping up at least once each generation. Her oldest pair of brothers were twins. Not the slightest doubt now remained in Tara's mind that Drucilla, like her own mother, had been born a Wentworth. Once she got home it would require only an airmail letter to England to verify this guess. But she was already convinced as to what the records would reveal.

Her basic quest fulfilled, she was content to skim through the rest of the pages. The household had long since settled down for the night. The only sounds in Kilgarrom were the rustle of paper and the booming of the grandfather clock on the landing downstairs. It had chimed twelve before she came upon Drucilla's description of Kevin's terrible death:

> *Seeing the life blood gush forth from my beloved, and knowing well my father's savage temper, I caught up my babes, one in each arm, and made haste for my bedchamber. Fortunate we were that this room was once a part of the ancient keep, for there a hidden entrance, twin to the door concealed in each turret, lay ready to hand. For three nights and three days we kept hidden in the passage, until in truth my sons near starved, and during that time there was naught but the harp, given me by my own Kevin Fitzgarth, to drive away the black horrors of insanity. . . .*

Shuddering from the vivid intensity of the words, Tara set the manuscript aside. How lucky that Caithlin had not read this account! Surely, it would have heightened to positive conviction her belief that Drucilla still restlessly roved the passage, playing her harp!

She glanced once more at the page, seeking a certain line. *A hidden entrance, twin to the door concealed in each turret,* she read. Rory had shown her the trick of gaining entrance to the turrets. What fun it would be to return the favor, and point out to him the latch in Drucilla's bedroom, kept secret all these years!

The desire to see if she could locate the hidden entrance, to gaze just once into the passageway where Drucilla and her sons had lain concealed, became a solid ache. If only she were not committed to leaving tomorrow!

Tara jumped up in sudden decision. Tomorrow she would be on a jet crossing the Atlantic. If she were to make the attempt at all, it would have to be tonight!

CHAPTER THIRTEEN

Tara moved swiftly before she had time to change her mind. Caithlin, she felt sure, would have no objection to her aim, but she herself could think of any number of reasons to postpone the plan. It was dark and cold and late—very late. They were all excellent reasons, counterbalanced by only one factor. Postponement would mean not later, but never. And always afterward, for the rest of her life, she would regret having turned aside from a taste of adventure.

She slipped on her coat and rummaged in her bedside table for the flashlight. Tucking this into her pocket, she picked up the kerosene lamp and stepped quietly into the hall.

Kilgarrom was totally dark. Even the candlelit chandeliers had been extinguished hours before. It was no wonder, Tara thought, that each bedroom was supplied with a flashlight! Being familiar with the castle's floor plan helped. She turned in the right direction and made her way to the master bedchamber at the head of the main stairway.

She had entered the room only once before. Going there with Eileen on the night of the seance, she had been struck by the extreme chilliness within its four walls. Then she had attributed the low temperature to the fact that no one had used the room for centuries. Now, though, as she pushed the door open and slipped inside, it seemed no colder than any other part of the house.

At once, she realized that locating a tiny, concealed latch was going to be no simple matter. It could be anywhere! Three large windows at the far end of the room looked toward the rear of Kilgarrom. She pushed aside one of the dusty curtains and stared out. The view of the kitchen garden and the forlorn little cemetery in no way helped solve her problem. She measured the thickness of the stone wall with her eye. Despite its unusual width, she doubted that there was space enough between interior and exterior wall to house a passageway such as the one Drucilla had described.

Tara set the lamp down on a bureau and maneuvered the wick until the flame was burning its brightest. What she wouldn't give for a few hours of bright daylight! Drawing the flashlight from her pocket, she turned for an inspection of the bedchamber's side walls.

Logic told her that the hidden opening must be concealed somewhere along in there. The partition between bedroom and corridor was far too thin even to consider. And at the rear of the room, windows interrupted the thick stone.

Rising on tiptoe, she stretched high then bent low, tracing careful fingers across every reachable inch of wall—with no result whatsoever. Much of the space was inaccessible, of course. The canopied bed barricaded a stretch of six or seven feet on one side of the room, while the heavy marriage chest prevented a section on the opposite wall from being thoroughly examined. Furthermore, her searching fingers came nowhere near the high ceiling. But Tara felt sure that Drucilla had been even shorter than herself. She couldn't have reached very high. Nor would she have placed furniture in the way of her escape route. The entrance must have been located where she could get to it instantly in time of emergency, slip through, and leave no trace of her exit for enemies to find.

Frowning, Tara sat down for a minute, trying to figure out how this could have been done. Quickly, that was for sure. With her father and his soldiers at the foot of the stairs, Drucilla had been able to snatch up her sons and bolt into the passage before the vengeful pursuers could overtake them. For more than seventy-two hours she and her boys had remained safely hidden while the English hunted for the secret opening. The catch must indeed be intricately concealed!

If in all that time they had failed to locate it, how could she hope to succeed? The only extra clue she possessed was the knowledge that this opening was identical to the one in the turret. But in order to manipulate the catch, she still had to find it. And so far her explorations had resulted in nothing but sore fingers.

About ready to admit defeat, Tara turned her gaze once more on the windows. The side walls and partition fronting the hallway were smooth to the touch. Back there, though, no paneling or plasterboard had been used to mask the rough texture of the original stone. Thoughtfully, she picked up the lamp and moved closer. True, the windows did interrupt the sweep of the wall. But the bottom sills were waist high. A tight crawl space could have been hollowed out beneath the panes of glass.

The massive gray blocks had been chiseled into rectangles, laid flush to stretch across the twenty-foot stretch of the wall. The stones used to erect the turrets had been set in a circular pattern. But that made no difference, Tara told herself. It was a crevice between the blocks where the answer should lie.

With mounting excitement she ran her fingertips along the lines of cement. Up, down, across, painstakingly feeling for a tiny catch invisible to the eye. When the blocks beneath the first window had been examined she moved on to the center, and finally to the third. Her efforts were in vain.

Between each window and on both end sections where the side walls ran down to form a corner lay a three-foot width of solid wall. The conviction that nothing would be found there either was almost too tempting. By now the skin of Tara's fingertips was ragged and torn from contact with the rough stone. She dabbed the blood off on a tissue and doggedly persisted in the chore, wondering what had ever made her regard this frustrating search as an adventure.

The left-hand corner yielded nothing, nor between the first and second windows did she discover anything but rough concrete. Sighing in discouragement, she bent to examine the solid space separating the second and third windows. A particularly uneven ridge of mortar took its toll. Blood traced across the stone, making her wince. She jerked back. As she did so, her thumbnail flicked a small, protruding node.

At first she was too stunned to believe her good luck. If her fingers had continued their downward course, they would have passed right over the spot, mistaking it for nothing more than another lump of imperfectly mixed cement. She reached out again, tentatively wiggling the minute projection first in one direction, then in another. The wall held, seemingly as impenetrable as a granite cliff.

Tara closed her eyes, concentrating on remembering the peculiar twist and thrust motion Rory had used to gain access to the turret. Imitating his movements to the best of her ability, she made one final attempt to probe Drucilla's secret.

The wall clicked open.

So startled that she fell back in a heap on the Persian carpet, Tara stared in total astonishment. A gaping hole opened where a moment before there had been only rigid stone. Scrambling up, she played the beam of her flashlight across the aperture. The hinged, three-foot-square section was quite large enough to admit a stooping adult. However, it did not lead to a mere crawl space inside the wall. Instead, a narrow flight of stairs, five or six steps in all, descended into the gloom.

Won't Caithlin be flabbergasted! Tara thought, giving full credit to the older woman. If she hadn't located Drucilla's diary, the secret opening would probably have remained hidden forever.

When deciding upon the venture, it had never been any part of her plan to explore the passageway. All she had wanted was the satisfaction of finding it. She was not at all fond of dank, cramped places. But shining her beam downward once more, she came to the conclusion that whatever lay below was not the tight, airless space she had been visualizing.

The passageway appeared to be a full-sized tunnel, suspended between the first and second stories of the castle. Since the ceilings of the downstairs rooms were at least twelve feet high, no one but a blueprint specialist would suspect that an extra layer had been sandwiched between the floors. Tara remembered how long both stairways had always seemed. Yet as often as she had climbed them, it had never occurred to her that there might be a special reason for this.

She drew the lamp forward to glow across rough-hewn walls and a rugged stone floor. This was no mere niche where a desperate person could hide. Most likely the passageway twined from one end of Kilgarrom to the other.

Satisfied, she started to withdraw the light from the opening. At that very moment its radiance sparked an answering sheen from below.

From where she crouched, Tara could not identify the object that had reflected the beam back to her. Metal of some sort, she concluded. Too bad there hadn't been pirates in Ireland, stashing their loot between battles. She would find no treasure chest of jewels and gold here. But there was something. . . .

Removing her coat, she bunched it around the corner of the opening to guard against the door snapping shut. Cautiously, then, she descended to the floor of the tunnel, and shone the lamp directly on the article that had piqued her interest.

It was a harp. Not the small Irish instrument, which can be held in one hand. A much larger sort. The kind used in orchestras.

Thirty or forty seconds ticked by while Tara blankly eyed her find. This wasn't the harp Kevin Fitzgarth had given his Drucilla. That was inside on the marriage chest. But in that case—

The implications began to dawn on her then. Of course, it wasn't Drucilla's harp. Yet someone— Neal's late-lamented Uncle Cormac, for a guess— had wanted Caithlin to *believe* it was a ghost she heard playing!

Tara had spent twenty-three years learning to control her temper. In less than a minute all this careful self-discipline unraveled with a snap. She had never felt more completely furious in her whole life. If Cormac were alive, she'd probably drown him herself. What a mean, wicked trick he had played on his wife!

So much that before had seemed baffling was now blazingly clear. The weird music echoing forth from between the walls, the footsteps "where no human feet could tread," even the sudden extinguishing of a light. When the Spiritualist Society had gathered downstairs beneath the portrait, the candle flame hadn't just puffed out. It had been blown out by a draft from this very tunnel. That was also what had caused Drucilla's bedchamber to seem so frigid.

Funny, Tara mused, that there was no draft now. The tunnel itself wasn't even particularly cold. Just stuffy and damp. A draft would have snuffed out her lamp, brought crisp fresh air whistling into the room.

As she stood there cogitating, the reason for this anomaly occurred to her. Somewhere—on one end of the tunnel or the other—a door had been left open the night of the seance. Whoever came through it had walked along this tunnel. He or she had operated the latch from the passageway to spring back the secret entrance to Drucilla's room, twanged a simple melody on the harp, then snapped the concealed door back in place.

But why?

A signal, of course, she realized immediately. Whenever Caithlin had heard the haunting notes of the harp and taken the melody to mean that Drucilla was still searching for peace, it had been only a signal for Cormac—a coded message in music rather than words, having to do with rifles and bullets ready to be smuggled.

But Cormac was dead. Who else might still be listening for such a sound?

Tara swallowed hard, sure now that her mounting suspicions had been correct. On the night of the seance there had been only one person awake in Kilgarrom besides Caithlin and herself and a group of total strangers. Eileen.

Eileen, who'd summoned Neal outside the night a boat had come drifting up from Lough Duneen. Eileen, who'd urged Tara to go away and do her research in Dublin. Who had stolen quietly to the back door with a conspiratorial message. Eileen, who with Neal had driven up to Belfast.

There was just one thing she didn't understand. That evening, when the party had been stunned by the "supernatural manifestations," Eileen had appeared to be genuinely terrified—as if she really believed in the Lady with the Harp. Eileen could be a superb actress, Tara admitted, but even an Oscar winner would hardly have almost dropped a kerosene lamp to achieve verisimilitude.

Tara gave the harp a scornful glare and stamped back up the narrow little stairway. Eileen could behave anyway she wanted, she thought indignantly, and—and Neal was a grown man. If he chose to stay here in Ireland to aid the rebels, she wasn't going to try to stop him. What made her mad— what she just wouldn't stand for—was seeing them take advantage of Caithlin!

Angrily she snatched up her coat and thrust her arms through the sleeves. The secret door hadn't budged. Still, she had no intention of trusting her life to it. A swift foray in her own room produced a handful of paperback books. With these she blocked the stone entrance so that even if the hinge weakened and the panel snapped shut, it would not close all the way.

What she intended to do now was find the door which, when opened, had created that draft. If contraband had been brought into the castle a few nights ago, it had no doubt already been transported across the border. Even so, some evidence of its transient stay might remain. This would be the last bit of proof she'd need to lay all the facts before Caithlin.

Let Inspector Sheridan do his own investigating, she thought mutinously. Even now she had no intention of betraying Neal. But she certainly did intend to let him and Eileen know that their secret entrances and elaborate code were no longer a secret. Once they realized that, Kilgarrom should be safe. They wouldn't dare use it as a way station again.

Leaving the lamp on the steps to serve as a beacon, Tara snapped on the flashlight and turned right, heading in the direction of the turret standing nearest the kitchen. The tower would make a perfect hiding place, she decided, even though her one brief glimpse of its interior that day with Rory had revealed nothing more unusual than cobwebs and dust.

Tara had ventured only a few yards along the passageway, however, when her path was blocked by a pile of rubble. Much of the ceiling appeared to have collapsed. Not recently, either, from the settled look of it. Broken stone blocks and heavy beams, all covered over by a silting of cement, composed a quite impenetrable barrier. She beamed her light at the ceiling. More loose rock clung a few inches above her head, threatening to become debris at any moment.

Not even a desperate smuggler would have tried to bypass this obstacle.

The harp player, then, must have come from the other direction. Making a wary U-turn, she retraced her route. The lamp burning on the stair was as welcome a sight as a valued friend. For many yards after passing it she could look back over her shoulder and catch sight of its encouraging rays. Then, abruptly, the floor of the tunnel began to slant upward. The cheery beacon faded from sight. Gloom closed thickly in.

Tara's progress was painstakingly slow. Her footing was none too secure. Twice she stumbled and nearly fell as a loose stone shifted under her weight. She kept a constant watch on the ceiling, also, ready to bolt at the first sign of an incipient cave-in. Most time-consuming of all was her search for a second stairway. Rory had told her that the inside of the turret nearest the precipice had been demolished by the landslide. Therefore, the door she sought must lead out from another of the castle's rooms, like the exit from Drucilla's bedchamber.

But a second narrow flight of steps was nowhere to be seen. And all the while the passageway-become-ramp was rising, climbing ever higher.

It was when Tara had begun to feel that she could not endure the thick, cloying blackness for another single minute that she came upon the door. Dead ahead of her, it filled the mouth of the tunnel in the same close-fitting way the blade of a guillotine snuggles into its gruesome frame. She wished that she was able to think of a more comforting comparison, but she couldn't. The door was ceiling-tall, wall-to-wall wide, ponderously heavy. And it had a handle—a rusty door-pull.

She backed away. Now that she had actually found the door, she didn't want to open it. She wanted to run away as fast as she could, back to the safety of her lamp and the spring-hinged panel stuffed with paperback novels. Supposing the guns were still there, just the other side of that door? Supposing Neal and Eileen. . . .

But if she turned around now, she would never know for sure. And all her life, even if she lived to be as old as Brigid, she would have to remember that she had been a coward. Her hand closed over the cold, pitted metal. She gave it an experimental tug. A crack widened, and a draft of chill, biting air whooshed across her face. Light blazed into her eyes.

Tara tightened her grip on the flashlight, squeezing until pain shot through her cramped fingers, until the impulse to scream receded. She had been expecting an empty storage room—a continuation of the tunnel's unmitigated darkness. Instead, torches, four or five of them, flickered high on metal brackets. Nor was she peering in at the cavernous expanse of the attic. The opposite wall was only twelve or fifteen feet away. It didn't slash straight across from corner to corner, like the wall of a room, either. This wall had been built eight hundred years ago, out of rough-hewn stone set in a circular pattern.

But Rory had said—

Whatever he'd said wasn't true, she realized, ten seconds later. Because Rory himself had just walked into view.

CHAPTER FOURTEEN

It was a perfectly preserved medieval tower, untouched by the effects of the landslide. In fact, the only difference between this turret and the one she had visited last week was the stack of long, sinister-looking crates on the floor.

That much Tara had managed to take in before Rory crossed her line of vision. For several minutes afterward she was too numb with shock to think of anything else. It took the chilling draft to at last jolt her from this spellbound daze. Her brain started working again. She found herself listening and watching, trying to make sense out of the scene taking place before her eyes.

Foolishly, after the trip to Belfast Tara had thought she'd at last begun to know Neal's cousin, to penetrate his sardonic shell and see the real person concealed beneath it. But she had been wrong. Here was a Rory she had never met. His intense expression reminded her of a general deploying his troops in the field. Gone was the sarcastic, mocking manner. Every word he spoke was an order, which the others in the tower accepted without question.

Besides Rory, she caught glimpses of at least six other men. They were working in pairs, each hoisting one end of a crate, straining to lift it knee high, then shuffling off with their burden toward the winding stairs leading down. She could hear muffled curses, scraping noises as a sharp wooden corner raked the wall, a jolting thud when they reached ground level. The first pair did not immediately reappear. Two others bent and repeated the same maneuver.

Apparently the work had been going on for quite some time. The men looked sweaty and spent, as though they had labored half the night. They were buccaneerlike in appearance, clad in dark jerseys and denims, some with kerchiefs knotted around their heads. This last bit of attire nudged her memory, made her think of burly men lazing in the sun while their womenfolk bustled around the wagons. Tinkers!

Rory did not stand idle. He shifted crates from the diminishing pile, shoving them forward one by one to where they could more easily be hefted and borne away. But there was never any doubt as to who was in command.

From her inch-wide slot in the door Tara could see only a small part of the shifting kaleidoscope of movement within the turret. Nor was the men's conversation enlightening, since the few words exchanged were in Gaelic. But it was easy enough to guess what they were doing. Kilgarrom was a way station, probably the last one before the weapons were smuggled across the border. In a very short time the turret would be empty, the guns en route.

Tara's cheeks burned with humiliation and regret when she thought how convinced she'd been that Eileen was in charge of the smuggling ring, and that Neal was helping her. The jolt of realizing her enormous mistake also triggered what was left of her common sense. Already she had lingered too long in this dangerous spot. If Rory or one of the Tinkers were to glance in this direction—

Her fingers tightened over the iron handle, easing it back toward its original position. But before the latch had clicked tight, two men struggling to lift an especially cumbersome load stumbled and crashed against the door. Their violent backward motion catapulted the heavy oak panel wide open, pinning Tara to the tunnel wall and jarring the flashlight out of her hand.

For four stunned seconds the only sound was that of the metal cylinder clanking and thumping as it rolled back down the inclined passageway. Then came the rush of bounding footsteps. Rory leaped over the fallen men, darted into the tunnel, and hauled Tara out from behind the door.

She was obviously the last person he had expected to find there. After a shock-still pause, he tightened his grip on her sleeve and dragged her out to the center of the turret.

"Couldn't my cousin finish his own spying?" His lips twisted in derision. "Did he have to send a girl to snoop for him?"

The harsh question acted like a slap across her

face. "Neal isn't involved in this, Rory. I found you
out for myself," she said, matching his scorn. Her
glance flickered across the splintered crate. "How
many women and children do you think those guns
eventually will kill?"

"No matter. Anyone who sides with the English
is an enemy," said one of the Tinkers, struggling to
his feet.

Rory silenced him with a curt gesture, then rat-
tled off a string of Gaelic which had the ring of a
command. Sullenly, both men bent to clear away
the smashed packing case. But the tension did not
abate when their backs were turned. Rory continued to eye her with a mixture of anger and exasperation. She wondered what he intended to do next.
A couple of the Tinkers wore sheathed knives at
their belts. Rory looked quite capable of turning
her over to them.

Amazingly, his lean face split in a sudden grin.
"Just like our Drucilla all over again," he said,
chuckling. "I should have guessed you'd have her
spirit, as well as her looks! She hid in the passageway for days, did you know that? Outfoxed the
British completely." He leaned forward, clutching
both her arms in a bruising grasp. "And now you're
going to help us do the very same thing."

Tara jerked away, not giving him the satisfaction
of an answer. She'd never help him—never!

Retreating until her back was rigid against the
rough stone wall, she tried to think of some way to
free herself from this grim situation. The secret entrance in Drucilla's bedchamber was still open; the
lamp beside the harp was as good as a signpost,
telling where she'd gone. When Neal came back,
all he'd have to do was walk up the main stairway.

He would be bound to see the light shining in the tunnel straight ahead, and come to investigate.

Almost before this thought was fully formed, the hope was dashed. Another pair of Tinkers trudged up the winding staircase. Rory dispatched one of them down the passageway with explicit instructions.

"If you're waiting to be rescued, don't," he said, turning back to Tara. "Screaming will do you no good, either."

Tara recognized the truth of his statement. The turret towered yards above Kilgarrom's roof. Even if the walls were not so thick, the bedrooms were much too far away for one brief shriek to reach their occupants. She knew instinctively there would be time for only one. Then she would be effectively silenced. Nor was it any use to hope that the flickering torchlight would be noticed by anyone outside. Each of the arrow slits was masked with black tar paper. Curling slightly at the edges, it looked as if it had been in place for years.

She nodded toward the covered arrow slits. "Cormac's idea?"

Rory grinned. "A clever man, wouldn't you say?"

"I would not!" Fury struck sparks in her flinty gray eyes. "What's so clever about deceiving a dear person like Caithlin into believing she's living with a ghost?"

"Is that all that's troubling you? Sure, and it did no harm. Neither Cormac nor I would do anything to hurt her. Caithlin was always superstitious. A ghost in the family just added a bit more interest to the castle. Besides, tales about Drucilla had been told for centuries. The Lady with the Harp was a legend. But policemen seldom trouble themselves with gossip about spirits. So when Cormac needed a signal, he just brought her to life again." Rory gazed thoughtfully toward the tunnel. "Later he had Drucilla's portrait taken to the attic. He was afraid she'd bring him bad luck."

Tara fought down a shiver. Cormac, too, had had a leaning toward the supernatural. Yet he'd played games with it!

"Cormac is dead now. You don't have to take orders from him anymore." She tried dissuading him from this terrible undertaking he was involved in.

Rory laughed at her. "Sure, and it's an adventure. The pay is good, make no mistake, but it's the excitement that I find so irresistible."

Just then the Tinker who had been sent to reconnoiter the tunnel returned. Tara's spirits drooped even lower as Rory took her books from the fellow and thrust them at her. "So you really did come alone." He gave her a mocking bow. "I admire your spunk, if not your intentions. Someday you must tell me how you found the hidden latch."

Tara lowered her eyes. Drucilla's diary was still on her bedside table. Perhaps in time another member of the family would page through it, and discover what she had learned. That wouldn't happen soon enough to help her. Nevertheless, she kept obstinately silent.

Rory shrugged and turned back to the work at hand. Even though carrying them away was a monumental job, the stack of crates had finally dwindled. The winding turret stairway had been built for archers and for armor-clad defenders, with the steps curved at an angle to give their sword arms free play. Tara couldn't help but reflect on how disgusted those early ancestors of the Fitzgarths would have been, had they known to what use their clever design would one day be put.

Rory was everywhere at once: dispatching, supervising, leaping forward to help when a load threatened to topple. Never again, if she lived to think about it, would Tara be able to picture him as the proprietor of a bookshop. This was his natural element.

Even under the present circumstances, she couldn't help noticing what an attractive man he was. Whipcord slim, tall and lithe in his black turtleneck outfit. But he lacked Neal's kindness, his concern for others. Tara found it incredible now that she could have so lost faith in her fiancé. If she had just stopped to think, instead of taking his actions at face value, her heart could have told her that Neal was no criminal. Instead she had accepted matters as they seemed to be, and so did him a great injustice.

When all but two of the crates had been lugged away, Rory returned to her side. "What a schemozzle this whole operation has been!" he said. "Nothing has gone according to schedule. First the boatmen couldn't land the guns because of you and that idiot hound. Then my car broke down and I didn't reach Kilgarrom in time to hear the harp signal. The Tinker caravan was late too. They should have come and gone while Neal was away at the livestock auction."

Tara frowned. "What do you mean—'because of me and that idiot hound'? One of your boatmen hit me over the head, and Gray Boy didn't even bark!"

"He didn't bark because Cormac had trained him

not to. Gray Boy was taught never to interfere with anyone who came or went by boat. The fools made a mistake when they attacked you, though. It riled the dog. He chased them back to the water and raised the devil's own ruckus. They had to hide out and return when everyone was busy with Caithlin's ghost hunters."

Good for Gray Boy! Tara thought. Because he hadn't raised an alarm while she was conscious, she had automatically assumed that it was Neal and Eileen—people he knew—who'd been down on the shore. Now it appeared that he had rushed her attacker and summoned aid with his frantic yelps!

"He also chased away one of your Tinkers last night," she added with satisfaction. "But why did you think Neal sent me to spy on you?"

"Ever since his arrival my cousin has been nosing into things that are none of his business—and Eileen helping him. Cormac's own daughter!" Rory sounded incensed. "They learned enough to feel certain that books were not my main interest, and that Kilgarrom was the base of operations. I was faced with an unpalatable choice. I had to agree to the sale of the castle and promise to bring in no more weapons, or they'd pass the word along to the *garda*."

Tara remembered the sheet of paper lying on the kitchen table between the cousins. Her eyes shifted to the last remaining crate of guns. "So you gave your word, then promptly broke it!"

Rory's laugh held genuine amusement. "Haven't you learned by this time that I am not an honorable man? In fact, I drove you to Belfast meaning to spirit you away for a few days to ensure that Neal caused us no more trouble. But you disrupted my plan by spotting Inspector Sheridan. It would have been challenging to kidnap you right under his nose. Still, I couldn't risk it."

So it was the Rover the policeman had followed, not the MG. How obvious it seemed now! "I thought you were my friend!"

The smile faded. Earnestly, he said: "You'd have come to no harm with me, Tara. I came very close to falling in love with you. If my cousin hadn't already put the stars in your eyes—" He broke off, his face hardening. "Be assured my friends have no such tender feelings. Cause us no problems, and you'll live to tell about this night. But even I might not be able to intervene in time if they suspect you're trying to betray us!"

With this warning still ringing through the turret, Rory motioned for one of the Tinkers to extinguish the torches. He glanced swiftly around, making sure the door to the tunnel was tightly closed and that no trace remained of their night's work. Seizing Tara's arm, he thrust her ahead of him then, down the narrow, spiraling staircase.

Books spilled unheeded from her hand as she struggled to keep her balance. Her one thin hope was Gray Boy, running loose in the courtyard. But this too was dashed when Rory pressed a spring-latched panel built into the side of the stair wall. It led not outside but down, along yet another tunnel.

The dank corridor must have been built for gnomes, Tara thought. Rory was forced to stoop low. Though a full foot shorter than he, she fancied she could feel the slimy rock ceiling brushing her hair. The rank atmosphere with its lingering aroma of perspiration and gun oil made breathing difficult. Nor did the jiggling flashlight beam always reveal hidden obstacles in time. One of the Tinkers preceding them stumbled, wrenching his ankle. Rory swore, mercilessly propelling the limping man onward.

When at last they emerged into it, the swirling gray mist was a clinging, cloying, almost tangible thing. Tara breathed in gratefully as drizzle sleeted across her face.

Rory shot an exultant glance at the low-hanging sky. "Just the weather we need," he declared, ramming shut the hillside exit. "We'll be well away from here before dawn breaks, and halfway to the border by the time this haze lifts. After that—who's going to stop and search a gypsy caravan?"

Only half of the wagon train was being used to transport the weapons, it developed. The slower vehicles were being left behind with the caravan's dogs and children and the majority of the women. A few females were coming along to furnish a natural appearance in case they did encounter anyone.

Tara had no intention of allowing herself to be made up as a Tinker woman to aid in the masquerade. If ever she were to escape, this would be the time to make her break. The gypsies were proceeding stolidly ahead; Rory's attention was for the moment occupied. She edged away from him into the thickness of the night. But before the wisping tentacles of mist could close between them, he quickly sidestepped and caught her shoulder in his rigid grasp.

"I warned you," he muttered through clenched teeth. "Since you won't walk beside me as a friend, you'll come as my prisoner!"

Tara mulishly stood her ground. "Family or not, Rory, I'll do everything I can to see you defeated.

You can't make me take part in this dirty business."

"We'll see." With an angry muscle twitching in his jaw, Rory hoisted her off the ground and slung her over his shoulder. Tara struggled frantically, aware that resistance to his superior strength was futile, yet refusing to concede that he had beaten her. In the brief flurry she managed to kick off one shoe without his noticing. Leaving that clue behind was a small triumph, but the best she could manage. Two minutes later Rory strode up to the assembled caravan and tossed her, still kicking and biting, into the nearest wagon.

His spurt of Gaelic to the two husky women inside sounded brusque and explicit. Before Tara could recover from the jarring impact, a gag had been slapped across her mouth, and her wrists were twisted and roped behind her.

"I'm doing my cousin a favor, taking you off his hands," Rory said, rubbing his forearm where her teeth had sunk into the flesh. "Behave yourself if you want to stay alive. These folk regard all foreigners as enemies."

He spun around and vanished into the mist, heading toward the front of the caravan without once looking back.

Tara had been abandoned to the gypsies. No one helped her sit up. She managed that feat by herself, only to be hurled backward again when the horse-drawn wagon lurched forward. A bruise on her cheek began to prickle. Splinters gouged her hands and legs. Doggedly she scooted around until she could brace her back against the upcurving side of the wagon.

At first the women regarded her with hostile suspicion. As time wore on, they lost interest and reverted to their usual habits. One dozed; the other stared vacantly ahead. The din of pans, kettles, and fire tongs hanging from hooks and clashing together as the wagon swayed and jolted across open fields made conversation impossible even had anyone been inclined to talk.

Little by little, Tara's eyes became accustomed to the gloom. Up front, the driver's stocky bulk on his raised platform blotted out any possible view. The shadowed interior of the Quonset-hut-shaped vehicle was jammed with household goods piled haphazardly atop the all-too-familiar wooden crates. The women had cushions to sit on. Their captive felt lucky to have landed on a clear patch of dirty floorboard.

The bare boards were numbingly cold. A blanket flapped across the back of the wagon, letting in drafts with every swaying motion. Tara concentrated on trying to see out whenever it swayed in the breeze. The few glimpses she caught in this way were far from reassuring. Seven wagons in all made up the caravan Rory was leading north. Hers was the fifth, leaving two more behind. The next wagon was only a few yards to the rear. She could see the driver alert on his benchlike seat up front, flapping the reins and peering ahead for signs of trouble.

Tara closed her eyes, shamming sleep, and behind her back started to work on loosening the ropes. It must have been two hours later that she began to hear the soft, rhythmic sigh of water lapping at a shore. Lough Duneen, she knew, must lie far behind by now. But Inspector Sheridan had mentioned a chain of lakes twisting north. She in-

tensified her efforts to free her hands. For count-
less minutes past she had been hooking a loop of
the rope over a nailhead jutting out an inch or so
from the wooden crate on her left. It was a painful
process, jerking her hands forward to fray the
hemp, but gradually the strands had slackened.
With an extra effort now she felt them give just
enough. Her wrists twisted and wiggled until finally
the scratchy rope dropped away. Prudently keeping
her hands behind her back, she massaged her
fingers until they began to tingle with life once
more.

The women, lulled by her apparent docility, had
long since ceased to glance in her direction. Even
so, Tara did not make the mistake of underestimat-
ing them. With the utmost care she shifted position,
moving to the rear of the wagon a fraction of an
inch at a time. Her right hand crept out, twitching
the blanket a hairsbreadth aside.

It was at that moment that the swaying motion
abruptly halted. Terrified at first that the driver had
somehow guessed her intentions, she froze. Then
she realized that the jangly din in the other vehicles
had ceased too. The whole caravan had jounced to
a standstill. A hoarse shout from up ahead caused
the driver to secure his reins and slide down off the
platform. Another twitch of the blanket showed
two more men lumbering past.

Tara wondered what had gone wrong. No matter; she would never have a better opportunity.
With all the men congregated at the head of the
wagon train, there were only the women to reckon
with. They also were gazing ahead in anxious speculation. She slid her feet sideways, toward the edge

of the opening, flipped aside the blanket, and leaped to the ground.

Tara had a few seconds' head start. Then a milling hubbub in the wagon she had left behind warned her that pursuit was imminent. She tore off her gag and jerked a frantic glance to the left. The mist was thinner now, wispier. Through its swirls she caught sight of a flat rocky field studded with white blotches of bog cotton. No cover there. And ahead and behind were the wagons.

She opted for the lake.

Stones notched her shoeless feet, slick grass sent her skidding; nothing stopped her. She was within two or three yards of the water, stumbling down the gently inclined bank, when a darting look to the side showed what had delayed the caravan. A rickety wooden bridge stretched ghostly gray across a narrow arm of the lake. But a section of it seemed to be missing. Already the lead wagon had begun a slow circle around the obstruction. All at once furious shouts bayed back and forth. On either side of the caravan flashlights stabbed through the night.

For a split second longer, Tara hesitated. Suddenly, above her head, a shot rang out. It hadn't come close, but the next bullet might find its mark. She hit the water in a shallow dive.

CHAPTER FIFTEEN

T he water was glacier cold. Tara gasped in shock, but her arms and legs churned instinctively onward. She had taken a score of long, pulling strokes toward the middle of the lake before her first blind surge of panic subsided and rationality returned. She forced herself to tread water then, while she surveyed her chances and tried to decide on the safest course.

Ahead, the mist danced low across the wavelets, screening the vista in an opaque shroud. It was impossible to tell how wide the lake was, or whether islands drifted along its center. Were it only half as broad as Lough Duneen, the iciness of the water would surely cripple her before she could reach a landfall. And with visibility so limited, she could easily lose her bearings, swim around and around in helpless circles until she drowned.

173

Already the outlines of the shore she had left behind were blurred and unreal looking. Radiating circlets of light still swooped and darted along the length of the caravan, but they seemed to be coming no closer. Nor had the shot that had sent her plunging wildly into the depths of the lake been repeated.

They didn't know where she was.

Tara slipped into a gliding sidestroke and changed course, heading south along the shoreline. So long as she kept moving she wouldn't freeze, but the danger of cramp was ever present in her thoughts.

She estimated that she had swum about fifty yards when a bulky shadow loomed ahead. Cautiously, in silence, she approached the cape jutting out from shore. Her feet touched bottom. Teeth chattering, she pulled herself up onto dry land. Here, the low headland was studded with bushes. Underfoot, sand alternated with coarse vegetation.

Tara crouched alongside the dubious shelter of a stunted tree. Her streaming slacks and blouse seemed to blot up the chill night air and draw it inward, clear through her skin. Death from exposure could come quickly here. Longingly, she peered down the beach at the approximate spot where she had flung off her coat.

The mist here on land was thinner than the marshmallow-cream curtain hovering over the lake. An occasional breeze puffed a peephole in the swirling wisps to allow her a glimpse of the gypsy caravan. She saw that the wagons hadn't budged an inch since they'd parted company. Odder still, the flashlight beams, rather than being fanned out in a search pattern, were now clustered together at the head of the train. Across the water voices rumbled. Loud voices with the ring of authority in their tone. Once it seemed a whistle shrilled, but that might have been the cry of a night bird.

Tara released her trembling clutch on the tree trunk. Something very peculiar was taking place. Rory was a keen, fast-thinking leader. By now he should either have deployed his men on a concentrated search for her, or ordered the wagons underway as fast as they could travel. Yet neither of those things was happening.

For another five minutes she continued to stare at the foggy tableau. All at once, powerful twin beams of light slashed across the landscape. A motor revved. Her heart pounded with eager hope. If the Jeep behind the headlights belonged to the police, then the ruptured bridge had been a trap, a way to halt the caravan long enough for the gunrunners to be seized.

Cautiously she fought down a triumphant shout. She'd been wrong before. Almost dead wrong.

Until she was absolutely sure she didn't dare show herself. Because an ugly thought had just occurred to her: Instead of the authorities, that motor vehicle could belong to a group of rebels, come to escort the smugglers through the hills!

Bending low so her outline would remain unseen against the stumpy headland, she maneuvered cautiously across the tiny cape, then crawled back toward the mystifying scene. Every few yards she paused to listen. Once a splash disturbed the lake's placidity. It might have been a fish.

Tara had reached the halfway point between cape and caravan when she noticed that one light had pulled apart from the others. It moved in a jerky procession from spot to spot, darting impatient jabs through the haze, disappearing at intervals, then winking into sight again. After a while she figured out what was going on. The person holding it was proceeding systematically from wagon to wagon, stopping to enter each one, then climbing out and going on to the next.

Shivering almost uncontrollably by now, she crept up parallel with the rear wagon just as the beam traced a last stabbing arc through the air, then dropped. In the predawn dimness the outlines of the man's form were too insubstantial to identify. All she could tell was that the figure had a hunched, discouraged look.

"Any luck?"

She jumped as a second man loomed up to join the first.

"It's no use; I can't find her anywhere. You don't suppose those devils—"

No one ever heard the end of that sentence. Tara leaped up, running on ragged stocking feet as fast as she could across the rocks and slippery grass to fling herself into the speaker's arms. The flashlight dropped unheeded to the ground.

"*Alannah!*" Neal cried, wrapping her small, damp shape in his engulfing embrace. "Oh, darling! I've been out of my mind with worry. I was afraid I'd never see you again!"

Tara's first thought upon opening her eyes the next afternoon was that the plane was going to take off without her. But it didn't really matter. Nothing mattered except the fact that she was safe and warm and back in her own room at Kilgarrom— and that Neal loved her. He had made that unmistakably clear on the way home. Even her sobbing confession that she had suspected him of smuggling guns had had absolutely no effect on the tenderness of his caresses.

"Sure, and what else were you to think when I carried on in such a way," he soothed her. "It was only the danger that kept me from telling you the truth. That and shame for my own family. I wanted to keep you safe, untouched by this horrid business. It was bad enough that you'd learned of Cormac's sordid death, but to know that my cousin, too. . . ."

"That wouldn't have made a shred of difference." Tara snuggled deeper into his arm. "I thought I had lost you to Eileen. She's so beautiful, and— Oh, Neal! I nearly went home without you."

He confided then that Eileen was engaged to a young attorney in Cork. Rather than blight his career, she had kept their marriage plans a secret, hoping that the scandal of Cormac's insurgent activities would have a chance to die down before the engagement was officially announced.

"Just before I arrived Eileen learned that the worst wasn't over yet. An old crony of Cormac's spilled the news that another shipload of weapons was due to arrive soon—and that their destination was Kilgarrom," Neal said. "Eileen enlisted my aid, knowing I was no more anxious for scandal than she. Together we started checking every port, every contact, until we got a rough idea of the timetable to be used and the route the guns would take."

Now Tara understood their need for secrecy. On most of the trips the two of them had taken, Neal actually had contracted for handcrafted items to be exported to America. But this was only a cover. Their main purpose had been to track down enough evidence to put an end to the smuggling.

"From the start we were almost certain that Rory was involved," he went on. "Eileen and I hoped that if we could confront him with solid proof and force the sale of Kilgarrom he would give it up—retire from active duty, you might say. Last week we found out about a certain boat that was due to cross Lough Duneen. Like almost everyone else, we'd been deceived into thinking the turret nearest the precipice had been wrecked inside by the landslide. So we hid in the other tower, waiting for the smugglers to arrive."

Tara grimaced. "And thanks to me, they were scared off and didn't return until the night of the seance. No wonder Eileen looked so frightened when she heard the harp. That signal was for Rory, not for her. She, too, must have been convinced that the castle was haunted."

Neal nodded. "Drucilla's ghost was the best clue of all, if only we'd recognized it in time. Finally, we hit on the idea of consulting an architect to see if we could locate the cache. The detailed drawings of the castle showed that a passageway must be sandwiched in between the floors. Unfortunately, there was nothing in the plans to show where the entrances and exits to it were located."

Tara remembered thinking it would take a blueprint specialist to notice the discrepancy in the castle's proportions. How stupid of her not to have equated that notion with the word "architect." If she had, she'd have known that Neal was telling her at least part of the truth, and not concealing a more nefarious reason for the trip to Belfast!

"You eventually did find the panel in Drucilla's room, though, didn't you?" she asked.

He smiled and drew her closer. "Only after you had shown me the way. You have no idea how hard it was to hear you talk about going home, and not be able to say a word to keep you with me. But Kilgarrom wasn't a safe place for you. So I stayed away, knowing I'd weaken if we met again."

After returning Eileen's car that morning and catching a ride home with a farmer, Neal had spent the remainder of the day in the stables, watching the castle through binoculars. "Rory didn't show up until after dark. I almost missed seeing him. He must have parked off the road, near the bottom of the hill."

Tara, too, had heard the noise of a motor while bidding Caithlin good night. But she had dismissed the sound too casually.

Neal went on describing events from his viewpoint. "When part of the Tinker caravan moved back to the south meadow, I knew the gypsies had to be involved somehow. Too bad I didn't wait a little longer. I'd have gotten a look at that hillside exit Rory opened for them. But instead I ran back to Kilgarrom to see what I could learn from the inside. That's when I found your door open and the lamp gone. The diary was on your table. I read the last page, then headed fast for Drucilla's room. By then I was too far behind. Even after I saw the bloodstain on the stone, it took forever to twist the panel open. I finally got to the turret. But Rory and the guns were gone—and so were you."

His face blanched at the thought of what might have happened to her. "I knew when I saw your books on the stairs that we'd been insane to try and stop the smuggling ourselves, just to preserve what was left of the Fitzgarth honor. Luckily, Inspector Sheridan was staying in Ballycroom. Once I got there—Cormac's old Morris has traveled its last mile, I'm afraid—I learned he'd spent months keeping tabs on my cousin. As soon as he heard my story he mobilized the *garda* for miles around. He was furious at me for leaving it so late, but he relented and let me come along when the police headed north to cut off the caravan. We took the bridge apart and were in position by the time the wagon train showed up."

"What a time I chose to escape!" Tara murmured ruefully. After an interval, she asked what would happen to the Tinkers.

"The authorities are going to try and resettle the women and children into a normal community. Not that they'll stay. The men are in for long jail sentences."

"And. . . ."

He read her thoughts. "Rory got away. In all the confusion he either slipped through the ring of Jeeps and hid in the hills, or took his chances in the lake."

"The lake, I'll bet. There was a splash."

"Well, either way his organization is completely destroyed. He's finished in Ireland. Are you sorry he wasn't caught? I know he treated you shamefully."

Tara shook her head. "All that happened a million years ago. I'm glad we won't have to testify or picture him caged behind bars. It's better for Eileen this way, and for Caithlin, too."

* * *

It really did seem long ago and far away, she thought, as she got out of bed and slipped on a long-sleeved dress to conceal the bandages on her wrists. At last they could all begin to look forward instead of back into time.

Voices drew her down the main staircase. Neal and his aunt stood in the entrance foyer. Caithlin had been given a carefully edited account of the previous night's events. In her opinion, her daredevil nephew was by now safely hidden on the Continent.

Neal took a letter out of her hand and waved it at Tara when she walked across the tile to join them. "It's from the real estate company. A hotel syndicate is interested in taking a look at Kilgarrom. It seems that castles are all in vogue with tourists."

"Spending a night in a place like this would make anyone's vacation," Tara said with a laugh. "Of course, they'll have to add any number of bathrooms and completely refurbish the place. Still, I've no doubt it would be a good investment."

"The legend is well known. Supposing they want us to leave Drucilla's portrait and harp and other things here?" Caithlin asked, looking faintly troubled at the prospect.

Soberly, Tara gazed up at the painting of her look-alike. "After all, this is the home she shared with her Kevin," she pointed out. "And Drucilla dreamed of Kilgarrom becoming the most lavish residence in all Ireland. The hotel chain will probably make that dream come true. Let her stay."

"I agree," Neal said.

The three of them stepped out into the courtyard. Tara reached back to pull the door shut. As she did so, she fancied she heard the lilting chords of a harp tune echoing down the stairs.

Then she smiled at such a nonsensical idea. Of course Kilgarrom wasn't haunted. Hadn't she proven that herself? *Of course!*

And yet. . . .